Sincerely Yours!

THE CONCLUSION

AL-SAADIQ BANKS

SINCERELY YOURS?

AL-SAADIQ BANKS

TRUE 2 LIFE PRODUCTIONS

SINCERELY YOURS?
All Rights Reserved © 2003 by True 2 Life Productions

For information contact:
True 2 Life Productions
P.O.BOX 8722
Newark, N.J. 07108
E-mail: true2lifeproductions@verizon.net
Author E-mail: alsaadiqbanks@aol.com
www.true2lifeproductions.com

Printed in Canada

ISBN: 0-974-0610-2-6

Fellas, I didn't forget about ya'll. I know ya'll expecting another hardcore joint, but I had to flip the script a little bit. The last two I wrote for ya'll. This one is for the ladies, but I'm sure ya'll will enjoy it as well. In the process of standing by our sides through our battles, lots of times they get caught up in the struggle too. They also make some wrong decisions. I can't forget about them.

Sisters, I dedicate this one to ya'll. Ya'll kept asking me to drop a joint for ya'll. Well here it is.

Keep ya headz up and stay true!!!!!!

Main characters from the previous volumes:

No Exit Part I
Tony/Nephew
E-Boogie
Du-Drop
Auntie
Reemie
Buck-Wild
Cool Breeze
O-Drama
JJ
Aisha
Tara
Flaco

Block Party Part II
Cashmere
Love
Slim
Desire
Ahmir
Ahmad
The Mayor/Junebug
Spook
Ice
Mike Mittens
Pretty Ricky

CHAPTER 1

February 7, 1999

Suave shakes the dice rapidly. He promises himself that this is his last round. Of course, he told himself that two hours ago, too. He wanted to leave a long time ago, but a strong force kept him glued to his seat. He's not sure if it's the money he's winning or the fact that he doesn't know how these guys will react if he leaves without giving them a chance to win back their money.

Tonight must be his lucky night. Normally, he leaves penniless. He's a heavy gambler, but he's no good at it. In fact, he hasn't come out on top in all the years he's been coming here. He's probably lost a couple hundred thousand dollars in here over the past four years.

Tonight his luck changed. He walked in with $2,500, and now he's holding onto approximately $40,000.

A few major players are in here tonight. All the big shots from this town gather in this tiny, hole-in-the-wall spot every night. They come from everywhere. Money that they have risked their lives and freedom for all day, they willingly put on the crap table at night.

The gambling hall opens at 11:00pm. Sometimes the games last until 6 or 7 in the morning. They play until every player is completely broke.

You would never imagine how much money is floating around in here. On a good night, close to $200,000 circulates through the room.

It's the perfect after-hours spot. Las Vegas has nothing on this joint. In here, you can get weed, liquor, and pussy. What more can you ask for? The owner makes you as comfortable as he can as he gets rich off your hard-earned money. He brings in at least five beautiful girls every night. The owner gets half of their earnings from the night on top of a hefty percentage of the winnings. The spot is an auto body shop in the daytime and a crap house in the late-night hours.

The chicks sure know how to make that money. They walk around ass naked the entire night. Just as fast as a nigga wins some money, he passes it off to one of the girls.

A combination of cigarettes, weed, and sex fills the air.

Tonight is a different type of night though. The girls aren't getting much action. Suave is holding onto the bulk of the money, and he hasn't even looked in the direction of the chicks. They all have tried some sort of tactic to get his attention, but they all have failed. Pussy is the last thing on his mind. He has his mind on one thing, and that's the pile of green that's laying on the table.

The dice land. "Yes!" Suave screams. "It's over!" he shouts, as he gathers all the money and pulls it toward him. In total, he collects $12,500.

All the players back away from the table one by one. Judging by the long faces, Suave can tell that they're broke. Some are broke only for the moment, but others are dead broke. Some of these guys put their last on the table, hoping for a come-up. Some are show-offs who gamble big money, knowing they can't afford it. Others are just addicted and will gamble anybody's money, knowing they will be in debt tomorrow. They'll even gamble the boss's money. They'll put their jewelry and car keys on the table. They get so caught up in the moment that they don't realize what they have done until they walk out that door and finally discover that their $15,000 watch is not on their wrist or the key to the $70,000 Mercedes is no longer in their pocket.

As Suave counts the money, the room is filled with tension. Damn near everyone watches him with hatred as he counts $52,500 out loud. Tonight is the luckiest night of his life.

Suave grabs a stack of money and starts to count it. He counts out $5,250 and passes it to the owner. He immediately starts counting again. He calls over to the kid that he won the majority of the money from. Of the $52,500, Suave won close to $30,000 from him. Suave breaks him off $6,000. He then hands $2,000 apiece to the other four players. Everyone's face looks a little more cheerful, except the girls.

"What about us, Suave?" one of the girls asks. Suave then reaches in his pile and peels off five $100 bills for each of them.

Suave gave back $21,750, leaving him with $30,750. The average person would not have given any money back, but Suave is not the average person. True indeed, he has a good heart and he knows that shows good sportsmanship, but he also realizes that it can be extremely dangerous trying to get out of this spot with all this cash. These dudes hate to see their last cash leave out the door in another dude's pockets. You never know which sore loser will meet you out front. He figures that by giving back a portion of their money, they'll at least have a head start on building some more capital.

Suave gives everybody the Peace and makes his way to the door. He's the first to leave. Everyone else is more or less doing their own thing. Some are rolling blunts. Some are back on the table, and others have disappeared into the back room with the girls, getting their trick on.

Once Suave gets to the entrance of the alleyway, he can see his car, which happens to be three cars away from him. He digs into his pants pocket and pulls out his car keys. He hits the alarm to his black on black Porsche Carrera. The lights flash on immediately.

He finally approaches his car. As he reaches for the door handle, a shadow appears from his right side. He turns his head quickly to the area behind his car. A figure pops up like a jack-in-the-box from between his car and the car that's parked directly behind his.

Suave's heart begins to pound rapidly. Suddenly, paralysis takes over his body. It's so dark out that it's impossible for Suave to see who it is. All he can see is the reflection of the long-nosed handgun, which is aimed at his head from five feet away.

"Don't move, nigga," the voice whispers. Suave is now fully aware of what's going down. A bunch of questions begin popping into his head. Who is this? Did one of the losers set me up? Did the owner make a phone call to have this guy waiting for me? Or was this guy just out here waiting for the first person to come out? Nah, he thinks to himself. This guy had to be waiting for me because he was sitting on the curb behind my car.

"Nigga, you know what this is. Get naked!" he shouts in a hoarse, raspy voice. He steps closer to Suave as he speaks. Suave is still frozen stiff.

"Hurry the fuck up!" he shouts, as he slides a bullet into the chamber and presses the nose of the gun against Suave's forehead. The gunman holds the gun with one hand and reaches inside Suave's pants pocket with his free hand. The gunman glances around quickly. Suave can sense fear. In fact, he's acting so nervous that he's starting to really scare Suave.

Suave's eyes finally adjust to the darkness. Now he can see the gunman's face clearly. Suave is positive that he's seen this guy before, but he's not sure where.

The gunman notices Suave trying to identify him. "What the fuck you looking in my face for? Stop looking at me! Turn the fuck around!" he shouts as he spins Suave around and places his forearm against the middle of Suave's back.

Suave is trying to remain cool and calm. The last thing he wants to do is make the guy more nervous than he already is. "Listen, calm down. Let me get the money for you," Suave whispers. "I'm about to go in my pocket, alright?" Suave asks as he digs into his right pants pocket and pulls out a hefty knot of about $1,200. Suave prays that this will make him happy and hopes he'll spare his life. Suave extends his hand slowly. "Here, take it."

"Where the fuck the rest of it at? Nigga, you trying to play me? I know you just scored big in there! Where the paper? Hand it here, or I'm a bust yo motherfucking head open! I ain't bullshitting!" he claims as he glances around nervously.

Suave now realizes that this is a life-and-death situation. This guy knows about the winnings. As much as he hates to turn over the money, he has to in order to walk away from this situation.

Suddenly, the gun crashes into the back of Suave's head, causing his legs to get weak. "Nigga, stop stalling! Give me the fucking money before I spill yo ass out here!"

Suave immediately fumbles in his pants, where he has the money stashed in a plastic bag. He quickly hands over the bag, trying to avoid another blow, or even worse, losing his life.

"Give me everything! Where's the watch?"

Damn, Suave thinks to himself. They even told him about the watch.

The gunman snatches Suave's watch off of his wrist. Getting his watch taken hurts more than the money. The $30,000 was never his to start with, but he paid $45,000 cold cash for his diamond-bezeled Ulysse Nardin. The watch means so much to him. It's part of a limited edition. They made only 500 of that particular model.

"Pass me the car keys, too."

Damn, not my car, Suave thinks to himself. "Come on, man. You got the dough and the watch. Not my car, please man," Suave begs.

Before he could finish spitting the words from his mouth, two back-to-back, excruciating blows crash against his skull. He then passes over the keys with no more hesitation.

"Now run!" he shouts. "Run before I murder yo ass out

here."

Suave stands there with a confused look on his face. "Haul ass," he shouts.

Suave trots off, feeling humiliated. This guy has his $80,000 car, his $45,000 watch, and $30,000 cash. The gunman really came off. He got him good, but he made one mistake. He never checked Suave.

After about three or four steps, Suave peeks over his shoulder to see exactly where the gunman is. The gunman has just turned his back and started to flee. Suave pulls his rubber-gripped Berretta from his waist and spins around. He has a clear shot at the kid. He fires. Boom! Boom!

The noise surprises the robber. He ducks his head down and peeks over his shoulder. Without aiming, the robber fires recklessly. Boc! Boc! He didn't shoot with the intent to hit anything. He just fired to keep Suave away from him. Now he's running for his life.

Suave fires again. Boom! This shot pierces the robber's thigh. The robber fires back without looking. Boc!

The wound has slowed him down drastically. He's almost dragging his left leg. Now Suave is gaining on him.

With about ten feet separating them, Suave squeezes the trigger again.

Bingo, this one hits the robber in the hip area, causing him to tumble forward. His gun escapes his hand as he rolls over. Now Suave is standing directly over him. He aims at the center of his chest and fires. Boom! By this time, sirens are echoing throughout the entire area. Suave has to flee the scene. He grabs the bag of money, then digs in the robber's pocket until he locates his watch and car key.

The sirens are getting closer. He fires once again before running to his car, leaving the robber laying there motionless.

Before jumping into his car, Suave takes one good look around the entire area to make sure no one is watching. The

coast looks clear. He jumps in his car and takes off at top speed.

CHAPTER 2

June 2000

The visiting hall is extremely crowded. The musty stench of jail mixed with cheap perfume creates a terrible smell.

This is Sincere's first time ever visiting a jail. All the frisking made her nervous. The corrections officers really have a way of degrading you. They even treat the visitors like criminals. The way they look at the women as they enter the building is humiliating. It's like they're looking at them with X-ray glasses on. They boldly look the women up and down and make sexual gestures at them.

The entire situation makes Sincere feel uncomfortable, especially the way the officer questioned her about whom she was coming to visit. He had the nerve to drill her about dating a convict. He told her she's too beautiful to be dealing with a prisoner and how she's cheating herself because she deserves better. He wrote his number down and demanded she give him a call, even after she clearly told him that she's madly in love with her *fiancé*, and there was no chance of her calling him. When she said the word fiancé he and two other officers laughed hysterically in her face. She was so embarrassed that she felt like running out of the building.

Her love for Suave is what made her take the disrespect. Despite what the officers said, she knows deep down that Suave is truly a good man. There's no doubt in her heart that he's the perfect man for her. She knows she has to ride this one out with him. She has to hold him down and be the trooper he expects her to be.

Suave hid out for approximately three months after the shooting before detectives found him. After a year-long trial,

Suave was finally sentenced to three years. This is only his first week on the inside -just the beginning of their nightmare. Sincere doesn't know what to expect. She's unprepared, even though he continuously schooled her on what to do if something like this were ever to happen.

She really never thought this day would ever come. She thought all of this was just a figment of Suave's imagination. She always felt like Suave was too paranoid. He always thought someone was watching him or out to get him. They couldn't go to the mall without him embarrassing her. The way he stared at every Caucasian was crazy. He thought every white man was a cop. He would get so nervous that his palms would sweat and he would start stuttering. She never understood it. She always thought he was overreacting. She didn't know why he would carry on like that. Little did she know, his mind was playing tricks on him. All his dirt and mischievous deeds were weighing down his conscience. Suave has been surrounded by negativity his entire life. The fast money, the murder, and the double crossing were just too much to keep concealed in his heart, especially considering that he never discussed his business with anyone. That made him a walking time bomb. No one knew when or where he would explode.

Suave is the only man Sincere has ever loved. They have been together for close to ten years now. She's against his lifestyle, but she knows that the streets are all he knows. He didn't even finish high school. He only made it to the ninth grade before he dropped out. She always begged him to leave the streets and go back to school.

Sincere truly believes that Suave could have turned out better under different circumstances and that he didn't have a fair chance. He has never seen his father. In fact, he doesn't even have a clue who his father is. His mother died when he was ten years old. She died while giving birth to Suave's twin brothers, who also died in the process.

After her death, Suave stayed with his stepfather, the

man who had raised him ever since he could remember. Two months after his mother's death, Suave's stepfather decided he no longer wanted to be bothered with Suave. One day before work, he dropped Suave off at his grandmother's house, just like he had done every day for years. The only difference is that this particular time, he never returned to pick up Suave. Suave's alcoholic/junkie grandmother was forced to raise him. She hated the fact that she had to care for him just as much as Suave hated to be taken care of by her. Suave stayed with her for four long years.

One spring day, Suave came home from school and found his grandmother lying in the middle of the living room floor dead with a needle stuck in her arm. She had overdosed on heroin.

From that day on, things went even more haywire than they already were. Suave was only 14 years old, with no parent or guardian. The state was in the process of shipping him to a foster home, when the mother of his best friend offered to take full custody of him.

At that time, that was the best thing that ever could have happened to Suave. He already was considered a member of the family. Him and James (Kilo) had been friends ever since kindergarten. She took him in and raised him just like he was her own. Everything she did for her biological son, she did for Suave. Suave lived better in their household than he ever had in his own.

As good as this may sound, it turned out to be a terrible environment for Suave. Kilo's father was a big-time drug dealer. He had it all; cars, houses, furs, and jewelry. He never hid anything from Kilo or Suave. His life was an open book. He often made business deals right in front of them. There was no doubt in their minds; they both knew they wanted to be just like him when they grew up. Little did they know, they would be forced to grow up sooner than they could imagine.

At age 15, Kilo's father put them on board. He started

17

them off by letting them make his deliveries for him. A few months later, he gave them their first package of cocaine. It was on from there; they never looked back. He laid down the entire blue print for them. He told them all they had to do was listen to him and the money would pour in. It did.

Two years later, Kilo's father retired from the drug game. Him and Kilo's mom bought a house in Atlanta and moved, leaving Kilo and Suave to fend for themselves. He left them the apartment and all his connections.

At barely 17 years old, they had to step it up and play grown-men roles. At first, Kilo was in charge because his father left him with a little more control of the business. That's how he earned the nickname Kilo. He plugged in with everyone in the town who bought cocaine. That's the kind of guy he is. He's a go-getter. If there's money out there, he will get it at any cost. As the business grew, the streets started talking. Everyone started treating the two of them like kings. Women came from everywhere to get a piece of the pie. Kilo fell victim. Girls have always been his weakness. The more money he made, the more women he collected. After a while, all he wanted to do was party with the women. He would disappear for days, and Suave would not know where he was. Even with him being away though, the show had to go on. Suave eventually took charge of the operation. He didn't cut Kilo out; he just called the shots and made all the decisions.

They ran the streets crazily for six years straight before Kilo ran into a problem and had to break out of state. They never lost contact though. They talked to each other at least twice a week.

Suave misses Kilo dearly. He has only spoken to Kilo once since he's been locked up.

Sincere, on the other hand, knows the importance of education. She is a college graduate. At the present, she's a Realtor, making $70,000 a year. That's not bad for a 24-year-old black woman, but that's mere peanuts compared to Suave's income. What takes Sincere all year to gross, Suave can net in a couple of months. He's definitely a top dog. He's in control. Besides the housing project he solely controls, he's also a big distributor. Everyone picks up off of Suave. That's the only way. If you don't pick up from Suave, then you can't make any moves. Suave's uncle will see to that. Uncle El- Amin is the enforcer.

You don't have to worry about Suave. He's the kindest and most generous guy you could ever meet. Some would call him a push-over. Sure, he may have got at a few guys who pushed him to the limit, but overall he's about his paper. His soft heart would have cost him his life a long time ago had it not been for Uncle El- Amin. El- Amin loves and admires Suave. In truth, he worships the ground Suave walks on. El- Amin will murder anyone who looks at Suave wrong. He's dangerous. Suave is the only person who can keep him calm; he doesn't listen to anyone else. He feels like he owes Suave the world because Suave has been taking care of him ever since he first came home. El- Amin continuously thanks him.

In the late 1960s El- Amin was a notorious bank robber/ murderer. By the time Suave was born in 1974, El- Amin already had served seven years of his 25-year sentence. He murdered an off-duty officer who tried to play hero in a bank robbery. At that time, El- Amin was only 19 years old. Rumor has it that was his tenth body. Some older guys had turned him out when he was about 15 years old.

While in prison, El- Amin supposedly murdered four inmates over the years. No one told on him because they knew what the consequences would be. Three of the murders were stabbings, but the last one he strangled with his bare hands. After the victim died, El- Amin torched him; that's why they couldn't get the fingerprints off the body. He's not only respected on the streets, but he's feared throughout the entire prison system. El- Amin Eaddie is a legendary name. He's an icon who is respected all over the land. The name *Eaddie* alone has opened up a lot of doors for Suave. That's the reason Suave holds his position.

El- Amin knows if it weren't for Suave, he would have been back in prison a long time ago. Without Suave, he would be nothing but a murderer. Thanks to Suave, he has now been home for eight years.

El- Amin hates the fact that Suave had to go to jail. It's been more than a year now since Suave shot the stick-up kid who attempted to rob him. Little did the kid know, Suave never moved without his gun. El- Amin always told him that it would be better to get caught with it than be caught slipping without it. When the stick-up kid waited for Suave to come out of the gambling hall, he got the surprise of a lifetime. Suave shot him four times. Miraculously, he survived. He even had the nerve to testify against Suave. El- Amin promised Suave that whenever and wherever he runs into the kid, he will kill him on the spot.

Suave found out weeks later that the owner of the gambling hall set him up. That mistake almost cost the owner his life but the owner and El- Amin made a deal. In exchange for his life, he agreed to pay off El- Amin and Suave. El- Amin went to the shop every morning and picked up $500. That went on for approximately eight months before the owner finally went out of business and moved down south.

"Damn, was that the only thing you could find to wear?" Suave gets aggravated as he looks Sincere up and down. She's wearing a tight-fitted, pink baby phat belly shirt that shows off her 36 Ds. Her jeans are so tight they look like she'll have to cut them off. Sincere has a beautiful shape, even though she's what most would consider a big girl. She's 5 feet 10 inches tall and weighs 175 pounds. She's tall and thick, with juicy thighs, wide hips, and a shapely butt. She doesn't have a bit of fat anywhere on her body. Her flat, washboard stomach looks extra tight today. Her navel ring just adds to her sexiness.

"You told me to wear something sexy."

"Yeah, I told you to wear something. You damn near naked!"

"Boy please, I'm not naked."

"Fucking stomach showing, titties hanging everywhere, and your hips about to bust out them jeans."

By this time, Sincere has caught the attention of everyone in the visiting hall. The women are looking her up and down and rolling their eyes with jealousy, and the men are looking at her in total amazement.

"Sit the fuck down," says Suave as he stares into the eyes of everyone who is looking at her.

"Do you like my hair? You didn't even notice it." Sincere has a jet-black rinse in her hair, which is cut in a short, wavy style.

As Suave stares at her, he begins to mellow out. Her glossy, full lips and gapped-tooth smile will break any man down.

"I noticed it," he admits.

"Well, do you like it?"

"It's alright, but you need to let it grow back. I don't understand why you would cut all that long hair anyway."

Suave hates her haircut. The jet-black rinse looks terrible against her yellow complexion. It conflicts with her hazel eyes. When he first met her, she had long, thick, sandy-colored hair that hung well past her shoulders.

"So what's the word?" he asks.

"Nothing much," she replies.

"Did they hit you yesterday?"

"Yeah, I saw everyone except Easy."

"He wasn't outside yesterday?" he asks.

"They told me he had just left right before I got there."

"How much did they give you?"

"They gave me $500 apiece."

"Alright, Easy will probably hit you today."

"I told them to tell him I'll be back today."

Suave left instructions to everyone who hustled in the projects. He told all of them to give Sincere $500 every Friday. He's renting the complex to them while he's gone. He's almost sure they'll pay because they know if they don't, they will have to deal with El- Amin, and no one wants to deal with him.

"So how are you? Do you know a lot of people in here?" she asks.

"It's alright. I know a few cats, but they're not on this side of the building. It don't matter because the majority of these guys already know me and what I'm about. They all try to start conversations with me, but I ain't beat. I answer them and keep it moving."

Suave is trying to make Sincere think he's alright, but she can tell he's stressing. It's written all over his face. His eyes tell the truth. He has only been in here for one week, and it looks as if he has lost ten pounds already. He definitely can't afford that. He's already tall, and lanky as it is. He stands 6 feet 3 inches tall and he only weighs 170 pounds. He looks sick compared to the rest of the oversized gorillas in the visiting hall. She's scared for her baby. She's afraid one of them will hurt him. She knows he can hold his own, but he's too small to be in here with these savages. Now is the perfect time for someone to hurt him -while he's in here by himself without El- Amin.

It's hard for her to look at him with this state gear on, but worse than that, the stubble of his beard is growing back. Suave normally gets a haircut every two days. Everyone considers him a pretty boy; that's how he got the name Suave. You would never be able to guess Suave's age. Judging by his little peanut head, youthful eyes, and smooth baby skin, he appears to be about 18 years old.

"I miss you, baby," says Sincere.

"I miss you, too," he replies.

"This is going to be the longest three years ever," she

whispers.

"It'll be alright. It'll be over before you know it. You can handle it; just be strong."

Sincere lowers her head and stares at the floor. Suave watches the giant teardrops fall onto the table.

"Sincere?"

"What?"

"Look at me," he whispers, as he touches her chin. When she looks up, the tears begin to drip down her face. "It's going to be alright. Do you hear me?" She's not responding. "Huh? Answer me."

"I hear you. I don't like seeing you like this. When I leave, I want you to leave with me."

"Stop crying. You're going to make it harder on me. You have to be strong and hold it down. You can do it, right?"

"Yeah."

"I know you can, because you're a trooper. If you can't handle it, let me know now. Huh?"

"I can handle it," she claims.

"Look me in the eyes and tell me," he demands.

She looks him directly in the eyes. "I can handle it."

"Now wipe your eyes and stop crying like a baby," he says with a smile on his face.

She wipes her eyes and puts on a smile bigger than his. She's fronting; she's smiling on the outside, but on the inside she's crying like a newborn baby. She's scared; she's scared to be alone at night. She hasn't slept by herself in almost ten years. Suave moved her out of her foster home when she was 16 years old. At that time, he was only 18 years old.

She was only 15 when they met. Sincere was a foster child. Her foster parents used to beat her severely. After Sincere showed him bruises all over her body, Suave encouraged her to run away. One year later, she finally took Suave's advice, and they have been living happily ever since.

Even though he's only two years older than she is, he

practically raised her. He's done a great job of teaching her how to be a woman. He encouraged her to finish high school and to go to college. He paid for her college tuition with hustling money. Suave is so proud of how she has turned out. He's the best thing that ever could have happened to her.

Sincere feels lost and helpless without Suave. This has been the loneliest week she has ever had. It isn't about the money; she makes $70,000 a year herself. She has plenty of her own money. She banks everything she earns because Suave pays all the bills.

After conversing for a few hours, the corrections officer screams out, "That's it people. That's it. Visiting hours are over."

Everyone prepares for their parting. They all conclude the visit by hugging and kissing.

Sincere squeezes Suave extra tight. She knows this will be her last hug until a week from now, so she tries to savor the moment.

This is the worse part of the visit for everyone -knowing it will be at least 168 long hours before they can see their loved ones again. Some women will wait faithfully for the next visit, but others will break the code of loyalty. Who actually knows which ones have kept it real and which ones have not?

"I love you, Suave!"

"I love you, too."

As she walks away, he stares at the beautiful view of her wide butt. The thought that it will be three years before he can touch her sexually again almost makes him want to die.

"Sincere," he yells as she gets close to the door. She turns around instantly. "Don't forget, hold it down."

She smiles and continues to step through the door.

As she disappears, Suave turns around. He lowers his head. As he's walking back, one teardrop burns his face as it drips. He quickly wipes it away before any of the other inmates can see it.

Three Hours Later

The rest of the afternoon is really stressful for Suave. Watching Sincere walk out that door makes it sink in. He's really in jail. He won't enjoy the sweet taste of freedom until three years from now. All he envisions is Sincere sleeping in the nude all alone. Then again, will she be sleeping alone he wonders? That thought almost drives him crazy. He's almost sure she won't cross him. He trusts her, but he also knows that three years is definitely a long time. He only has one week in. They have 1,088 long days and lonely nights to go.

By now, everyone is doing whatever it is that they do every day. Some are playing cards, some are watching music videos, and others are doing push-ups. The majority are lying about how much money they made when they were on the streets. They even lie about the types of cars they had. They lie day in and day out. They weren't getting any money, and they weren't driving shit. The majority of them were dope fiends on the street who got locked up for some young niggas' dope, and they're taking the weight for it. If they weren't dope fiends, then more than likely they're locked up for some petty shit like stealing cars. One particular dude, Rahiem, has three years in and four more to go. They gave him all that time for stealing cars. He's a young, dumb motherfucker. Being that he's from out of town, he thinks no one knows what he's in there for. All he talks about is flipping kilos and shooting motherfuckers. He doesn't have a clue that an officer already pulled his card. He never did anything but steal cars and joyride.

Suave is a different kind of cat. He just sits around and

observes everyone. He hasn't said ten words this week. He never brags about the money he made. His motto is to let the streets tell your story. If you're somebody or you were doing big things, you won't have to tell about it; the streets will tell it for you.

By 9 o' clock everyone has made it to their cells. Suave's cell mate is some 50-year-old dude. Neither of them say a word to each other. They both act as if they are in there alone.

Suave doesn't know his name or what he's in for, and he really doesn't care to know. It appears that the old dude feels the same way about him. Not speaking makes the time crawl by, but Suave refuses to make friends with any of the inmates. He didn't come here to make friends. He just wants to do his time and get it over with.

CHAPTER 3

One Month Later/July 2000

Suave feels a little more comfortable around here now. He's no longer the new guy. Almost 70 guys have checked in after him.

The first month, he called Sincere three times a day. Now he's down to calling her just once before lights out. That's his way of checking on her and making sure she's home at night. At first, she cried every night when she talked to him, but now she's alright. She must be getting used to the situation.

One month has gone by, and Suave still hasn't held a conversation with a single person.

It's Friday evening at 8:30, which is almost time for lights out. Today was a very tense day in the day room. Suave felt a bad vibe all day long. Flex and his crew had been staring at him the entire day. When they thought he wasn't paying attention, they would huddle up and start whispering.

Flex is a huge motherfucker. Basically, he runs this side of the jail. No one wants problems with him. He's 6 feet 5 inches tall and weighs a solid 260 pounds. He's the strongest man in the entire prison. They have his bench press recorded at 525 pounds. He has one of the best-built bodies in the prison -no fat, just solid muscle. He's also the ugliest one in the prison. He looks like a monster with a superhero body. He keeps a crew of young jokers with him who move at his command.

As Suave leans over the rail watching two older men play chess, he sees out of the corner of his eye a small gathering to the left of him. Flex is in the center of the circle. The crowd disperses, and Rahiem walks toward Suave. Rahiem sits on the rail right next to Suave. Suave looks at him and slowly turns back to the chess game. Suave tries to act normal, but his senses tell him something isn't right.

After about three tense minutes, Rahiem stands up and speaks.

"Fam, what size are those boots?" he mumbles nonchalantly as he stands side by side with Suave, putting his boot parallel to Suave's as if he's comparing sizes.

"I didn't hear you. What did you say?"

"I said, what size are those boots?"

"My boots?" Suave asks innocently.

"Yeah, your boots!" Rahiem shouts. "Yo fam run them boots," he whispers as he looks from side to side to make sure the officers aren't watching. He then pushes Suave against the railing. As Suave stumbles backwards, he notices Flex and his boys sitting off to the side watching.

Suave bends down slowly and starts to untie his boots. As he unties the first boot, Rahiem speaks.

"Yo, hurry the fuck up!"

Suave moves a little faster. First he takes off the left boot and then the right. Once he has both boots fully off, Rahiem bends down and reaches for the boots. Clap!

Suave uppercuts him. Rahiem stumbles backwards. His nose is leaking blood. As he stands there holding his lip and shaking his head trying to shake off the dizziness, Suave swings one of the boots at him. Thump! That one bangs him across the left eye.

Thump! He bangs him across the forehead. By this time, Flex and the crew are on their way over. The noise has interrupted everyone. Everyone on the tier has stopped what they were doing.

Suave swings the boot three more times. All three land on top of Rahiem's head.

Rahiem falls to his knees. Before Suave can swing again, Flex and his crew have him surrounded. Suave spins around and presses his back against the wall, preparing to rumble. One of the kids swings a bolo at Suave, but Suave slips it.

"Yo! Back up. Everybody back up!" an officer screams. "Clear this shit up!"

They reluctantly back away from Suave -all except Rahiem. He's bent over on one knee and bloody as can be.

As the officer stands between Flex and Suave, Rahiem finally stands up. His left eye is closed shut.

"Everybody to your cells. Lights out."

They all start to walk away. Suave stands there as Flex backpedals away from the crowd. He's wearing a devilish smirk.

Once Flex gets into his cell, Suave bends down to put his boots back on.

"Baby boy," Flex shouts. "It ain't safe no more."

Suave doesn't respond; he just walks to his cell.

This is what they were planning all day long, Suave thinks to himself.

Suave walks into his cell and climbs up to his bunk. His roommate is sitting there looking at a magazine. After a few moments of silence, the old guy speaks. "Young'en, I don't know if that was a smart move," he mumbles.

"What?"

"That move may cost you. Those boys are dangerous."

"Yeah, well I'm dangerous, too."

"I'm not doubting that, but what I am saying is this. I don't know you. I don't know who you are on the streets and what you may have done, but what I do know is you're not on the streets no more. You have to watch them boys. Whether you know it or not, they run this side. They got time in; you're a new jack. If it comes down to niggas riding with them or riding with you, who do you think they gone roll with? I feel your courage and all, but you have to learn to avoid certain beefs if you expect to make it around here."

Suave just lays there staring at the ceiling. Not one time

has he uttered a word. He replays the situation over in his head.
   The cell mate interrupts his thoughts. "Young'en?"
   "Huh?" Suave replies.
   "Keep your eyes open," he whispers.

CHAPTER 4

The Next Day

It's Saturday afternoon -visit time once again. Suave can't wait to see Sincere. Last night, he didn't get a chance to call her, because of the commotion.

He couldn't sleep last night. Every time he dozed off, the words "keep your eyes open" would awaken him. He thought about it. Maybe he did make a bad move, but what was he supposed to do? Was he supposed to let Rahiem take the boots? Nah, he couldn't do that; that would have created an even bigger problem. He knows if he had allowed Rahiem to take his boots, he would have given everyone else the green light to do whatever they choose to do to him. That would have been the beginning of his ending.

Suave hasn't seen Flex or Rahiem all morning. That's a problem. He knows they must be planning something.

As Suave walks into the visiting hall, he glances around the crowded room. Not only is he looking for Sincere, he's also looking out for Flex. He doesn't see either of them. The table they normally sit at is empty. Where is she, he asks himself.

"Ay!" shouts a voice. Suave looks around. "Over here!" Suave looks to the left of him. There sits El- Amin. Suave walks over to him and sits down.

"Where is Sincere?"

"Damn boy, you ain't seen Unc in over a month and the first thing you ask me is Where is Sincere? What happened to 'Damn Unc, I'm so happy to see you'?"

"Damn Unc, I'm so happy to see you," Suave replies sarcastically. "Now, where is Sincere?"

El- Amin chuckles. "She couldn't come today because

31

she had to work. She said she waited for your call so she could tell you but you, never called. I told her niggas probably stealing your phone time," he says in a joking manner.

"Picture that," Suave shouts. "I couldn't call because I had to go in this young boy's shit last night. Punk motherfucker had the nerve to tell me to run my boots. Me, Suave. He gone tell me to run my shit!"

"What did you say?"

"I ain't say nothing. I just went straight in his shit!"

"You were supposed to. What happened after that?"

"Nothing. The C.O. stepped in between me and them."

"Them? Them who?"

"His crew."

"Who are they?" El- Amin asks. He's getting pissed at the thought of someone trying to step to Suave.

"I don't know," Suave replies, trying to brush off the conversation. "So, what's up with my lady? Do you be seeing her out? Is she fucking with anybody?"

"Suave, cool out. You gone drive yourself crazy worrying about her. Always remember a bitch gone be a bitch. No disrespect, but they gone do what they want to do regardless. One thing about pussy, you can't miss what you can't measure. Whether you in here or on the streets, if they want to cheat, you can't stop them. Don't look for shit. You got enough shit to worry about right here. Worry about this time you have to do. Suave, I know it's rough, but you have to adapt to the situation. Later for the outside world; you ain't on the outside. Just concentrate on getting into this bid. Do the time; don't let the time do you. Before you know it, it'll be all over. I know it's rough in the beginning, but look at it like this. One day this whole situation will only be a memory. You'll get over this obstacle just like you got over all the past ones that you've encountered in your life. I'm telling you some good shit! You know I know how to jail. I did 25 years with nan bitch by my side. If Sincere stands by your side, that's good, but if she don't, that's cool too. You'll get over it. This is a test for her. Look at it like a way to prove her loyalty to you. You took care of her all that time, spoiling the shit outta her. Now you'll find out if she was worth it or not."

"You right," Suave admits. Suave sits quietly as he absorbs the drink El- Amin just dropped on him. Suave truly appreciates the advice.

"Do you know if they paid her yesterday?" Suave asks, trying to change the subject.

"Yeah, she said they hit her."

"How about Easy?" Suave asks.

"Yeah, he paid her," El- Amin replies.

"Did he hit her for the whole month?"

"I don't know about that."

"He playing games. I been in here for five weeks and this is his only week paying her," Suave states.

"Oh yeah?"

"Yeah," Suave replies.

"I might have to pay him a little visit."

"Yeah, you might have to," Suave agrees. "So what's up with you?"

"I'm alright. I'm eating a little something something. I still got old girl pumping my shit across town. I ain't getting no major money, but I'm paying the bills," El- Amin admits.

"That's cool," says Suave.

A shadow appears in the doorway. The darkness catches Suave's attention. It's Flex. Suave's heart beats a little faster. Flex sits at the table close to the door. He's sitting with two small children and a fat woman who is uglier than he is.

"That's one of them right there," Suave whispers.

"Where?" El- Amin asks as he looks over the room.

"Right there by the door."

El- Amin glances over the entire room until he sees the huge monster by the door. As El- Amin looks him over, he and Flex happen to lock eyes. "Who? That ugly motherfucker over

33

there?"

"Yeah, him," Suave replies.

El- Amin and Flex continue to stare at each other. Neither one of them is blinking. El- Amin slowly turns his head. "Fuck that big, dumb motherfucker! He probably ain't nothing but a big pussy," El- Amin mumbles.

As El- Amin speaks, he looks over at Flex again. They lock eyes instantly. El- Amin puts a slight frown on his face to intimidate him. Flex slowly stands up from his seat and begins to walk toward them.

"This big nigga is about to get fucked up in here. Here he comes," says El- Amin.

Suave watches him as he awkwardly walks toward them. His knock-knees rub as he walks.

As he's approaching them, El- Amin slides his seat back and stands up. Suave follows his lead.

Flex is finally there. El- Amin and Flex stand face to face, or more accurately face to chest. Flex is about a half a foot taller than El- Amin. Size has never mattered to El- Amin. He has the heart of a lion. Even in El- Amin's older years, he's still as tough as nails. He's a little, quiet, old joker, but he can make a lot of noise. He's what you call a quiet storm. He has an intimidating persona. You can look at him and tell he has time in. Here it is in the new millennium and he's still wearing a hi-low, push-back- type haircut. The front is low with about four waves in it. The further it gets to the back, the thicker it gets. The top is flat until it gets to the peak, where it begins to round off like an afro. The sides are faded close. That's how the old-timer prisoners from the 1970's wore their hair. That haircut and his thick, overlapping mustache without a beard is a dead giveaway. Anyone who sees that haircut knows what it represents.

All the inmates are staring; they can sense the tension, and the word has spread around the prison already.

"Amin!" Flex shouts. "El- Amin, what's up?"

El- Amin doesn't reply. He can't place Flex's face.

Flex is smiling from ear to ear. The tension is broken. "You don't remember me?"

El- Amin tries to place his face, but he can't figure out where he knows him from. "Nah," El- Amin replies. Suave sits down.

"Fu, Fuquan!" Flex shouts.

El- Amin still doesn't have a clue who he is.

"Fuquan Lexington!"

"Fuquan Lexington?"

"Yeah, Rahway! I was down Rahway with you!"

"You was down Rahway with me?" El- Amin asks while pointing to himself.

"Yeah, I was there with you for a year before you left. Remember, you stopped them old heads from getting at me my first day there?"

Now it's coming back to El- Amin. "Oh, for sitting in my man's seat?"

"Yeah, yeah!" He grins. "Them old motherfuckers wanted to kill me!"

"They were going to kill you," El- Amin claims.

"I was scared to death. You remember?"

"Hell yeah, I remember. You was a little puny motherfucker then. How much did you weigh when you came down there?"

"I don't know. I had just turned 18. I was about 6 foot 1, weighed 155 pounds. I was a little nigga."

"Yeah, I remember you. How long you been down here?" El- Amin asks.

"Six years."

"What are you in here for now?"

"The same shit."

"Psstt!" El- Amin sucks his teeth. "How long you got left?"

"I'm short. I should be going to see parole in about a

year and a half. I know they gone give me a hit. I stay in so much shit," he claims as he glances at Suave.

"Hmphh," Suave snickers.

"What's up with you though?" Flex asks.

"Nothing much. I'm chilling, just trying to stay out the way," El- Amin replies.

"Yeah, I bet."

"Yeah, I'm a old motherfucker. What else can I do?" he asks sarcastically.

"Yeah, alright! Tell somebody else that shit. I know better than that, Killer-Min," he says with a smile.

Killer-Min is what they called him in Rahway.

"Killer-Min," Flex repeats, trying to kiss up to him. "Is this your family?" Flex asks as he points to Suave. Suave looks him dead in the eyes with no response.

"Yeah, this my nephew." El- Amin debates about whether he should or should not get on him about pushing up on Suave, but he knows Suave will get pissed if he does. Besides, El- Amin doesn't want Flex to think they were discussing him like he's a problem or something.

"Oh, yeah?" Flex asks with a stupid look on his face. He's expecting El- Amin to mention the beef.

Flex extends his hand to Suave, gesturing for a handshake. Suave looks at his hand as it dangles in the air. After staring at his hand, Suave looks him in the eyes. Flex slowly draws his hand back.

"Amin, it's good to see you again. I would love to sit here and kick it with you, but I have to get back over there to my family."

"Oh, alright then," Amin shouts.

"Amin, I'll be touching down real soon; is it alright if I get your number from him?"

"Yeah, do that."

"Alright, for sure," Flex shouts as he backpedals away from them.

Amin sits down. "That was one of the softest motherfuckers in Rahway -a straight bitch. My niggas wanted to murder him. I felt sorry for him because he truly didn't know better. He was a stunt dummy with thick bifocals on. He just got mixed up with the wrong crowd. Him and his homies got together and robbed a kid for a leather jacket. They souped his dumb ass up to shoot the kid," he explains. "I guess he got tired of niggas down Rahway extorting him, so he probably started hitting the weights, figuring if he got his weight up, jokers would leave him alone. That way, he could do his time in peace. That's usually how it goes. Niggas get all big so they can use that as a form of intimidation. Deep down inside, they're hoping no one calls their bluff. They ain't nothing but big pussies hiding behind all that muscle. I ain't never been into that lifting weights shit. I went in 145 pounds. At 145 pounds, I was more dangerous than the majority of the big niggas down there. I bet you he won't say a word to you now. On the real, we need to hook up with him."

"Fuck him."

"Nah, you don't have to fuck with him in here. Wait till ya'll get on the outside. We can use his big dumb ass."

"Use him for what?"

"Use him for the stunt dummy he is. He'll do whatever we tell him to. He just wants to be down. He'll be our stunt dummy. After I pump a little bit of heart in him, nobody won't be able to tell him shit. All I have to do is bust a couple of asses in front of him, show him how it should be done. Before you know it, he'll be a beast. All he needs is the right backbone to push him."

"Man, fuck him," Suave shouts.

For the rest of the visit, Flex continuously watches El-Amin and Suave in admiration.

After the visit is over, Suave immediately picks up the

phone to call Sincere, but all he gets is the answering machine. That infuriates him. His mind immediately starts to wander. A million crazy thoughts pop up in his head. He hates to think this way, but he can't help himself. He tries to block out the thoughts by repeating the words El- Amin told him "A bitch gone be a bitch."

He tries to put Sincere in the back of his mind, but the vision of her and another man appears clearly in his head. He wishes he could take El- Amin's advice, but he realizes it's easier said than done.

CHAPTER 5

March 2001

Eight months have dragged by. As for the outside, things are going fine. Everyone is playing their position. Each of them has been paying Sincere weekly, without delay.

Things with Suave and Sincere are alright but not the way he expected them to be. He finally realizes that it's his life that's at a standstill, not hers. He hates to call her and find that she's not there; that bothers him the most. After bringing that to her attention, she explained to him that she has been doing a lot of overtime over the past couple of months. She isn't doing it for the money; she only does it to keep her mind occupied. That's the only way she can keep her mind off of him, she says. She tries to reassure him by telling him whenever he can't contact her at home, he can call her office collect. Ever since then, each and every time she isn't home he calls her office and she's right there, just like she said she would be.

As for the inside, Suave hasn't had another problem. Flex does everything in his power to get in good with Suave. In fact, Flex spends his entire day trying to impress Suave. And it's not only Flex; everyone tries to be under him, even the corrections officers. A few of the officers know El- Amin from Rahway. That makes things a lot easier for Suave. He has more movement than the inmates who have been on the inside for ten or more years.

Everyone treats him like a superstar, especially the older inmates who know El- Amin personally. All day long, they talk Suave to death. They tell stories of all the wild shit Killer-Min used to do. Some stories even shock Suave. When Suave was a kid, El- Amin hid certain things from him. He didn't want

Suave to glamorize his lifestyle. Never did Suave imagine Amin doing some of the crazy things they say he has done. Even when Amin was locked up, Suave's grandmother lied to him about his uncle's charges. She told him El- Amin had gotten caught in a mix-up. He didn't find out the truth until he grew up and hit the streets. The streets told him differently. They told him that funny Uncle Amin was really Killer-Min.

Suave is so tired of hearing stories about El- Amin that the majority of the time he stays locked up in his cell just to avoid everyone. That doesn't even work. Sometimes he looks up and there someone is, ready to talk. They even nicknamed him Amin. Suave hates that. He wants to be his own man with his own identity. They expect him to be like his uncle, but he's totally different. He isn't a killer or a bank robber; he's a money getter, not a money taker. A few guys know him from the street, and they know what he's about, but more people know El- Amin and what he's about.

The old guy (Suave's bunkie) went home a week ago. He and Suave had just begun to open up to each other. Suave came to find out that he was also a fan of El- Amin, but he was just as dangerous in his day. Suave found out from Amin himself that the old guy was official. If Amin puts the stamp of approval on someone, then he has to be the real deal, because Amin respects only a few legendary names.

Although Suave was happy to see the old guy go home, he didn't want him to leave. Suave knew that was selfish of him, being that the old guy had just finished a 15-year sentence, but Suave and the old guy had formed a bond. Suave actually developed a little love for him.

After watching him leave, Suave promised himself he wouldn't get close to his next bunkie. He doesn't want to go through that again.

With the new Bunkie, this is unlikely to happen anyway. This guy is from the federal side of the jail. Everyone except Suave knows him already. He has almost ten years in on a 60-

year sentence. To make a long story short, he's never going home.

He doesn't talk much, not even to the people he knows. Him and Suave never hold any long conversations. They don't have much in common. All he does all day is read his Qur'an. Everyone calls him Good Muslim. He leads all the Muslims and gives the speeches at the Friday services. Suave doesn't like to talk to him because all his conversations lead to the Qur'an or Suave coming to one of the Friday services. Of all the bunkies, Suave had to get stuck with a newwave Malcolm X.

Suave would rather be cell mates with him than one of those other dick-riding guys though. If he were bunkies with one of them he would never get any sleep. You should have seen how hard everyone was trying to get into Suave's cell when they found out the old guy was leaving. Everyone wanted to be in the cell with little Amin.

CHAPTER 6

One Month Later/April 2001

Another month has passed. Suave is now ten months into his bid. The repetition is starting to drive him crazy. It's the same thing, day in and day out. The other day, he decided to do something different. He decided to start working out to keep his mind off the streets and to alleviate some stress. He also wants to build up his body. No one gave him a reason to feel threatened, but he's tired of looking at his skeletal frame body compared to the other inmates.

Suave doesn't know where to begin. He can't even do 10 push-ups. The other inmates damn near fight each other trying to be his personal trainer. Each day, someone new steps up and tells him something else to do.

Today is his sixth day working out.

"Come on, pull yourself up!"

"Aghh," Suave cries.

"Come on!"

Suave is on the chin-up bar, doing pull-ups. He hates these the most. When he first started he couldn't do one, but today they push him to do five at a time.

"Come on, you wasting time! Somebody else has to get up there."

Suave begins to inch up. "Aghh!" he screams.

"That's right, that's right. Pull up baby! Get money! Get money, nigga!"

Suave psyches himself up. He doesn't know where the burst of energy comes from. He pulls himself up. His chin is well above the bar.

"Six!" the inmate shouts. Suave drops down and slowly

pulls himself up again.

"Seven! Eight! Nine! Get money!" Suave is dangling in the air. His shoulders feel like they're on fire. His hands are numb. The blisters on the palms of his hands are swelling. His forearms are pounding. The veins in his neck are pulsating. As he tries to pull himself up, he's shaking like he's having a seizure. "Come on motherfucker!"

"Aghh!" Suave cries.

"Come on, if you don't hurry up, you're going to owe me three more."

"Ahh," Suave sighs.

"Come on, pull up baby! Pull up!"

Suave pulls. His arms are getting weak. His wrists feel like they're separated from his hands. He doesn't know how he's still holding on.

"Squeeze and pull! Squeeze and pull!"

"I can't squeeze. I can't even feel my damn hands."

"Motherfucker, pull! What the fuck do you mean, you *can't*?"

"I *can't*!" Suave shouts.

"Alright then, get down you bitch ass nigga!"

Suave is pissed at the way he was just disrespected. He squeezes the bar as tight as he can and pulls. "Aghhh!" He pulls himself up over the bar and freezes in the air. "Aghh motherfucker, you a bitch!"

The inmate smiles. "Get down, motherfucker!"

Suave lets go of the bar and lands on his feet. The inmate gives him a high five. "Good money!"

It's now his turn to get up on the bar. He jumps up and grabs the bar. As he's in the air, he stretches his arms out as far as he can. Just when it looks like he can't stretch any further, he slides his hands across the bar a little wider. He has his arms stretched out like they're rubber bands. It looks like it's going to be impossible for him to pull up with his arms stretched out this wide.

"One, two, three!" He pulls up so gracefully. "This that back money!" he shouts. "The wider the better! Seven, eight, nine. This is how you build a big back! Twelve, 13, 14. Peep my form. My legs are straight. I'm not doing the Harlem shake like you were," he brags. "Seventeen, 18, 19."

It's true. His form is beautiful. As he pulls up, every muscle in his body flexes. His abdomen looks like he has eight bricks inside, ready to rip through his skin. His chest bounces every time he comes back down. He's looking straight ahead. His face is blank. His eyes are fixed at the wall.

"Thirty one, 32, 33."

He isn't even breathing hard. He's not straining or shaking. He's still going at the same pace he was when he first started. You can see his skin stretching. Red stretch marks extend from his chest to his shoulders.

"Thirty eight, 39, 40!"

He's still going.

"Form, check out my form. I can do this all day," he brags. "Forty three, you dig? This ain't shit! I'm getting money! Forty-four, 45! Aghh!"

After the 45th one, he hangs on the bar.

"What's up?" he asks sarcastically. "You want some more? How many more do you want? Forty-five more, 100 more? Huh? Tell me."

He begins to pull up again. "One! Let me know how many you want! Two! Say it. Three! I'm about to show you who's the bitch. Four! For every ten I do, you owe me one. Six."

"Hell no! Stop! You better stop! I ain't doing no more. I'm telling you, you wasting your time."

"Twelve, 13, 14, 15."

"Chill!" Suave grabs him by the waist and drags him off the bar. They collapse onto the floor. He gets up playfully and tries to jump back on the bar. They're laughing hysterically.

"I'm going to show you which one of us is the bitch.

Watch out!"

"Nah!" Suave knows he can go forever. No one in the prison can do more pullups than this guy can. In here, he earned the name Monkey Man. They compare him to a tree-climbing monkey.

"You called me a bitch, so from now on when we're working out, I'm going to bring the bitch out of you every time. I'm a break you, mark my words. Now come on. Let's hit the dip bar, then we're going to do a couple sets of pushups."

"Come on man, damn!" Suave shouts.

"Ah, ah, I told you I'm going to break you. You fucked up when you called me a bitch. Ha, ha, ha!" he laughs satanically.

After a half hour of excruciating pain, the workout is over. Suave's entire body aches.

As he was taking his shower, he couldn't even wash his back because he could barely lift his arms.

Right before the phones cut off, Suave places the collect call. "Hello?"

"Hello!" she shouts.

"Sincere!"

"Yeah, what's up baby?"

"Nothing much. What were you doing?"

"You miss me?" Suave asks.

"Do I!"

"How was your day?"

"Tiresome! I'm already in the bed."

"By yourself, I hope!" he answers sarcastically.

"Stop playing."

"You better be by yourself."

"I'm not by myself. I have my little friend in bed with me."

"Yeah, right!"

"I'm for real."

"Yeah, okay!"

"Seriously," she laughs.

"Tell him to say something then."

"Alright, hold on."

Suave hears a noise in the background. "Did you hear him?" she asks.

"What was that?"

"Listen." He hears the noise again. "Hello!"

"Yeah, what was that?" he asks.

"What does it sound like?"

"It sounds like an electric razor."

"Nah, it's not a razor. That's already trimmed," she teases.

"What is it then?"

"It's my little friend."

"I know that ain't no vibrator."

"Yep."

"Swear to God?"

"I swear."

"Turn it on again. Let me hear it."

She turns it on again. This time, the noise is louder than before, like she has sped it up.

"You serious, that is a vibrator. Do you use that?"

"I'm about to."

"You crazy! Go ahead, let me hear you."

The noise starts again. This time it sounds off continuously. Sincere is completely quiet for a moment. "Sssss," she whispers. "Ooohh, oohh," she moans. "Aghh, oh my God! Ungh!" Her voice trembles as the noise continues in the background.

Suave is getting excited just listening to her. He pictures her laying there naked with her pussy soaking wet. The thought of that makes him feel jealous because he can't be there with her enjoying the moment.

"Oh, Suave!" she shouts. "Suave?"

"What?" he asks.

"Baby, I'm about to come! I'm about to come," she whispers.

"Me too, baby," he whispers as he strokes himself through his sweatpants.

"Oooh!" Her voice is trembling. "This feels good. Suave, I'm about come. Please come with me," she whispers. "Here I...."

Click! The phone goes dead. It's nine o' clock. At nine, the phones shut off automatically.

Damn, Suave says to himself. His dick is as hard as cement. Just to think that Sincere is laying there climaxing right now. Now, he's really jealous. His lady is laying there with a toy up her ass, and he's stuck here not even able to please her.

He slams the phone down and walks to his cell, where he falls asleep mad.

He awakens two hours later. He can't sleep. For once, Suave realizes he can't do anything for her. He's scared she might have to find someone who can. The thought of that makes him toss and turn all night long. All he can do is pray that she's there by herself and that she doesn't decide to call someone over to finish the job.

CHAPTER 7

Ten Months Later/February 2002

The prison is extra busy today. Besides it being Saturday, today is commissary day. This is the day everyone gets their food packages and supplies.

Suave always gets the biggest food packages. Sincere makes sure of that. Suave eats better in prison than most guys do on the streets. Not only does Sincere send him a hefty package, but she also sends four equal-sized packages to him using other inmates' names. In return for the favor, he feeds them throughout the month. He doesn't have to; he just does it out of the kindness of his heart. He feels sorry for some of these guys. Some of them have ten or more years in with no dealings from the outside. They have no friends, no family, no nothing.

Prison is just like the street. The rich niggas eat while the poor niggas starve. Suave always made a way for the poor niggas to live. He's been doing that the majority of his life on the street. The only problem is that in prison, there are more poor niggas than rich niggas. Even some of the cats who were doing them on the outside get on the inside and turn to poor niggas. It's impossible for Suave to feed everyone.

In prison, every man fends for himself. He has to do what he has to do to eat. Some work, some steal, some gamble, but the majority extort the weak. *Pushing up* is what they call it. Every inmate knows at least one other inmate who is weak and scared to be there, so the aggressive inmate promises the weaker one protection in exchange for food and money. That's how more than half of these guys survive their entire bids. Suave hates to see these weak individuals get pushed up on, but what can he say? It's a living for those guys. As the song says

"You can't knock the hustle."

Flex and his crew are making their rounds throughout the tier. Each one has his own team of "shook ones" who faithfully stock them with food. Some even get their loved ones to put money in these guys' accounts. Then collectively, everything is turned over to Flex, and he makes sure everyone eats and smokes throughout the entire month.

At the present, Flex is leaving a kid's cell. He has so much food he can't carry it all himself. Flex and his protégé Rahiem have to make two trips.

The kid they just visited is from down south. He goes by the name Richie Rich. This kid has a lot of paper. He's from North Carolina, but he got caught on the New Jersey Turnpike with a kilo of heroin and four kilos of cocaine. He had just come from meeting his connection in New York. He was near the last exit on the turnpike, just a few minutes from Delaware, when state troopers pulled him over.

The judge tried to finish him, but his lawyer cracked the case. The average joker would have been finished for life, but not Richie Rich. He got away with four years. The prison rumor is that he paid his lawyer $200,000 for the case. Do the math; $70,000 for the heroin, $125,000 for the cocaine, plus $200,000 for the lawyer. That's a total of $395,000. It's easy to see why they call him Richie Rich.

In his town he's the man -untouchable but he's a long way from home. Up here he's nothing but a meal ticket. There are only two ways to survive; either you pay up or you lay up. Most choose to pay up.

CHAPTER 8

Later That Same Afternoon

    In the visiting hall, not only does everyone treat Suave like a king, but they also act as if Sincere is the first lady. All the inmates who know Suave make it their business to come over and speak to her. Some of them even introduce their wives to her. They do anything and everything to get in good with Suave. Even the corrections officers give Sincere special treatment. For example, she doesn't have to wait in the long line. They rush her right in.

    Over the months, Suave has gotten used to the fame, but since last month things have gotten worse. Some kid from Suave's project complex just got shipped to Suave's side. He informed everyone of who little Amin really is. He told them everything. He boasted on and on about Suave and told them Suave is one of the richest cats in the town. He named each of the cars Suave owned and even told them about the shooting that landed Suave the three-year bid.

    Sincere looks extra special today. She's wearing a fitted, pinstriped business suit, and she's wearing her hair long, the way Suave likes it.

    Suave watches in admiration as she steps like a stallion through the corridor. But anger fills his heart as he sees one of the officers speak to her. As she walks past the officer, he begins to follow her. Once she gets to the entrance of the visiting hall, the officer disappears.

    "Hey baby," she shouts.

    "What did that cop say to you?" he questions.

    "Huh?"

    "Don't huh me. What the fuck did that cop say to you?"

"What cop?"

"The cop in the front. I saw him talking to you."

"Boy, he complimented my shoes."

"And what did you say?"

"I didn't say anything."

"What did you say, thank you?" he asks.

"I didn't say anything, not even thank you."

"I saw you," Suave lies. He's testing her.

"You didn't see shit because I didn't say shit! Everytime I come here, they have something to say."

"Something like what?"

"Nothing Suave, nothing. Forget I even said that."

"Forget it? Hell no, I ain't forgetting shit! What the fuck do they have to say to you?"

"Nothing, just slick ass remarks."

"What kind of remarks?"

"Please Suave, just leave it alone," she begs.

Sincere doesn't want to tell Suave the things they say because she knows how he will react. She doesn't want him to do anything stupid and get into trouble.

"I'm not leaving shit alone! What do they be saying to you? Do them motherfuckers know you from somewhere?"

"No!"

"Then why are you protecting them?"

"I'm not protecting them. I'm protecting you. I don't want you to get into any trouble with those officers," she whispers.

"Yeah, alright."

"Now let's start this over. Hi baby, how are you?"

"I'm alright," Suave mumbles.

"Speak up. I can't hear you!" She raises her voice.

"I said, I'm alright!" he shouts.

"Can I have a hug?" Suave reluctantly stands up and embraces her.

He barely hugs her until she tightens her arms up. He

51

can't resist her. He squeezes tighter and tighter until he feels a tapping on his shoulder.

"That's enough," the white officer whispers.

Suave stares directly in his eyes as he slowly sits down. "This motherfucker," he mumbles under his breath.

"Suave, stop," Sincere whispers.

"Do you have something you want to say to me?" the officer asks.

As badly as Suave wants to say something, he knows he can't. He bites his lip in order to keep his mouth shut. He knows this isn't the time or the place to talk back. He hates having someone talking down to him or disrespecting him in front of his lady, but he knows he has to swallow this one.

From that moment on, the officer stands against the wall directly behind Suave. Suave feels so uncomfortable, he can barely say what he wants to say to Sincere. The officer makes the visit seem long and tense. The officer knows he's making Suave feel uncomfortable. He hasn't taken his eyes off of their table -not one time.

"Time's up!" the officer screams as he looks directly at Suave as if he's referring only to them.

Suave is pissed off. He can't even kiss Sincere good-bye. He holds her hand, with the officer paying close attention to their every move. He's watching them like he thinks she's going to pass something off to him.

"Pssst!" Suave sucks his teeth.

"Psstt what?" the officer asks.

"Suave, go ahead back," says Sincere. "I love you!" she shouts, trying to take his mind off of the officer.

"I love you, too," Suave mumbles.

Sincere starts to walk away. Suave watches her ass jiggle after every step she takes. Her booty looks extra loose in those dress pants. After about ten ass-jiggling steps, she turns around. "I want that nappy hair cut off by the next visit."

Suave laughs.

"I'm not laughing. I'm dead serious."

Suave has his hair in twists, and his beard is growing thick and course. Sincere hates it, but Suave told her he's not letting these guys cut his hair. As of right now, he hasn't had a haircut or a trim in a year and a half.

Suave and the officer stare coldly into each other's eyes as they slowly pass one another. The officer laughs sarcastically in Suave's face.

Suave gets so pissed that he has to bite down on his bottom lip in order not to say something that he will regret later.

"Niggas run the street, but police run the prison," he mumbles under his breath as a reminder of where he is and what he's dealing with. He knows that it's impossible for him to come out a winner in this situation.

CHAPTER 9

Two Days Later

Suave and the members of his workout team are crowded around the pullup bar. They are watching as Suave gracefully does 25 pull-ups.

Over the months, he has gotten so much better with his pullups. Right now, regular chin-ups are nothing to him; they're too easy. He has to tie a chain with a 35-pound plate attached to it around his waist just to make it challenging.

As he drops down from the bar, one of his teammates takes the chain from his waist. He exchanges the 35-pound plate for a 45-pound plate. He then ties it around the waist of Monkey Man. Monkey Man jumps up on the bar as if the weight isn't even on it.

"One, two, three!" they all count aloud as he pulls up. "Ten, 11, 12!" He pulls up without fatigue. "Twenty three, 24, 25!"

After 25, he switches the program. He changes from pulling his chin to the bar to placing the back of his neck onto the bar. "This that shoulder money!" he brags. "Four, five, six!" Everyone watches in admiration as he pulls up 19 more times. "Twenty five! Yeah!" he shouts. "That's 50!"

The other inmates idolize them when they're working out. They wish they could pull up like Monkey Man's squad. Only one other crew works out as hard as Suave and his group, and that's Flex and his boys. He makes sure he breaks them down. Every session ends in muscle failure. After recreation time is up, they can't even lift their arms.
Flex knows he works them too hard, but he has to. Who would fear them if they were little, scrawny motherfuckers? If no one

feared them, how would they eat? They use their weight as a form of intimidation. Flex always tells them that their bodies are their tools. He says barbers have clippers, singers have their voices, a lawyer has his mouthpiece, and we have our bodies.

Right now, he has them in what is called the soul train line. A soul train line is a line of dumbbells with about two feet between each set. The first set they work with is 45 pounds, then the next is 60 pounds, and the final set is 75 pounds. As soon as a man drops the first set of dumbbells, he instantly grabs the second set and then the third. After each person goes forward, they work from 75 pounds on down.

"First you bulk it up, then you cut it up," Flex shouts as he works his way upward. He's not using the weight they use. That's not enough for him. He warms up with the 80-pound dumbbells, and then he goes to the 100-pound dumbbells. "Eight!" he shouts. "Somebody get the 120s ready. Nine! I'm just warming up! Ten!"

As soon as he drops the 100s one of his teammates passes him the 120-pound dumbbells. He curls them one by one.

"Four! Grrrrr," he growls. "Five, grrrrr. This is what I'm talking about. Six, grrrrr."

He's straining so hard the veins in his neck are ready to pop out of his skin. The average joker can't lift 120 pounds with two hands, and he's curling it with one hand. He's as strong as an ox.

"Nine, grrrrr."

"Get it, baby!" Rahiem shouts. "Get it!"

"Ten, grrrrr! Money!" He then slams down the weights and peels off his shirt. He looks like a beast, the way he's staring at every inmate one by one. He's enhancing the intimidation. Beads of sweat drip from his entire body. Veins are popping everywhere. His biceps are swollen and visibly pulsating.

After Flex's two minutes of fame, everyone focuses their

attention on Monkey Man, who is getting back on the pullup bar. Everyone watches with undivided attention.

"Twenty- seven, 28," Suave counts.

Clap!

The loud clapping sound echoes across the recreation room. Everyone stops what they're doing. All heads turn in the direction the noise came from, which is the area where Flex and his crew are.

"You a hardheaded motherfucker!" Salaam shouts.

Flex stands there holding the side of his jaw. He has a shocked look on his face. Salaam just bitch slapped him.

Salaam is a little dude. He only stands to the middle of Flex's chest. Salaam is an old head. He's about 55 or 60 years old. He's short and skinny with salt and peppered hair. He's so skinny he looks like a sickly old man.

Salaam has 18 years in the building. He's quiet, but he's extremely dangerous. Never does he converse with anyone who is not in his cipher. The majority of the inmates have never heard him say a word until now.

"Take that slap as a warning," he yells as points his index finger in Flex's eye. Flex stands there humbly without saying a word.

Rahiem stands up and starts stepping toward Salaam. As soon as he takes his first steps, every Muslim surrounds him.

"Stay in your lane. Rahiem," shouts a young Muslim.

"I don't have a lane, I'm a reckless driver," Rahiem shouts back.

"Be careful; don't get in my lane cause I'll take your life. I'll run you right off the road," the Muslim replies.

"Flex, listen," Salaam instructs. "Listen to me because I'm never going to repeat this ever again. Are you listening?"

Flex nods his head slightly. No one has ever seen Flex bitch up like this. Fear is written all over his face.

"Listen carefully." Salaam pauses. "Anyone who comes into this building reciting the words Ash hadu an la ilaha ill

Allah, they're with me."

Richie Rich comes out of his cell and starts walking toward the circle.

"You see him right there?" Salaam asks as he points to Richie Rich. "He's one of mines. Back up off of him."

"As Salaamu Alaikum," Good Muslim (Suave's cell mate) shouts as he steps into the circle. "What's the problem?"

"There's no problem, Ak," Salaam shouts.

"Well, let's clear this up then," Good Muslim whispers. Everyone steps away from the circle.

"That was my final time telling you," Salaam whispers to Flex as he walks past him.

Just as the crowd is dispersing, the white officer who Suave despises walks in. "What's the problem?" he asks.

No one replies. The officer's face turns red from embarrassment. He turns his face toward Suave. "What the fuck are you looking at?"

Suave looks over his shoulder to see whom the officer is talking to.

"I'm talking to you, motherfucker! Don't look over your motherfucking shoulder."

Suave is trying not to lose his cool even though he's getting aggravated.

"What the fuck just happened?" the officer asks Suave.

"I don't know what you're talking about."

"Look boy, I'm going to ask you one more time. What the fuck just happened?"

"I said, I don't know what you're talking about."

"Alright then, let's see if you know what I'm talking about after you get out of lockup."

"Lock-up? Because I don't know what happened?"

"Don't talk to me. Now I don't know what you're talking about!" He storms away as Suave and the crowd stand there dumbfounded.

Later That Evening

It's 11:00 p.m. The Goon Squad has just awakened Suave. That squad consists of nine big, redneck officers. They all stand at least 6 feet 5 inches tall, and they're as wide as two men put together. The tenth one is a short, stocky black man who stands only about 5 feet 6 inches tall. He looks like a midget compared to the rest of them. He has the most mouth out of all of them though. He's the only one doing the talking. "Get up before they have to scrape you up," he demands as he drags Suave onto his feet.

"Alright, I'm getting up. What the fuck did I do?" Suave asks without a clue.

No one replies.

Suave looks over to the black officer and reads his badge. "Officer Jones, what's up? Don't let them do this to me," he begs. "I didn't do nothing. We're both black. Don't let them do this to me. It ain't right!"

"I'm not black, I'm blue," he yells, referring to the color of his uniform.

Right then, Suave realizes he's fighting a losing battle. He closes his mouth and walks to the basement with his nine and a half escorts.

Meanwhile, more than 100 miles away, Sincere is standing in front of the mirror drying herself off. The sound of an old school club song fills the room. Tonight is a big night. Sincere and her best friend Mocha are on their way to an industry party. Mocha's special friend invited her to his album release party.

Mocha is the most scandalous friend Sincere has. She's a money-grubbing hood rat. Cathy is her real name, but once she got older, she started calling herself Mocha. She says the name Cathy is so old school, and it doesn't fit her image. Now everyone, including her mother, calls her Mocha. She and Sincere have only one thing in common, and that's the fact that they grew up on the same block, right next door to each other. When they were children, Sincere's mother did everything in her power to keep them apart, but it still didn't work. It was as though they were destined to be together. Overall, Mocha is a good person but when it comes to a nigga, she has a totally different attitude. She has no love for the opposite sex. It's all about getting hers. She's cold- hearted and self- centered. If you can't do for Mocha, then she has no use for you.

Mocha has never worked a day in her life, but she wears clothes from the latest designers, and she always has a brand new car. She has her own apartment, and her bills are never late.

Dudes love Mocha. Rumor has it that the "head" is off the hook. She stays in the middle of some ghetto drama. She'll tell them in a minute, "Ain't no ring on this finger. I don't belong to either of you." Yet they break their necks just to please her and outdo her other acquaintances. She controls their minds.

Mocha is very high maintenance. She adds points to a player's credit report. If a dude has a chick like Mocha on his resume, he won't have a problem getting any other chick he wants.

Although Sincere needs to unwind, she really doesn't want to go. Mocha literally had to beg her. She hasn't been anywhere since Suave has been away. She knows he'll kill her if he finds out she went to a party, especially with Mocha. He hates her the most. He even banned her from the house. He doesn't want Sincere anywhere near Mocha. He calls her a hoe-ass groupie.

Mocha returns to the house. She walks in with a brown

paper bag in her hand. She starts bopping hard to the music that is playing.

Mocha is so sexy. She stands about 5 feet tall, and she's fully stacked. She has the complete package. She's small up top, but she has ass everywhere. She has long, jet-black hair; smooth, ebony skin; and big, deep dimples. Mocha is what you call a heartbreaker.

As Mocha steps through the bedroom doorway, she looks over at Sincere, who is standing in front of the mirror fully naked. She's applying gel to her wet, wavy hair, which hangs well past her shoulders.

She watches Mocha through the mirror. The look in Mocha's eyes makes Sincere feel slightly uncomfortable.

Mocha non-discreetly looks Sincere over from head to toe.

Sincere suddenly feels shamed. "What?" Sincere innocently asks.

"Nothing," Mocha replies. "I thought you would be dressed already. We have to get to stepping." She pauses before speaking again. "Sincere?"

"Huh?"

"You are really beautiful," Mocha admits.

"Shut up, girl! You just trying to persuade me to go with you to the party. I don't know though. I really don't want to go."

"Nah, I'm serious. You really are beautiful. Any man would be lucky to have you."

"Not any man, Suave!" Sincere shouts while smiling, revealing the big gap between her teeth.

"I know, I know! Girl, you gotta get Suave off your mind. You gotta make Sincere happy. I'll be damned if I be sitting around waiting for a nigga to come home from jail. Shit! I wish I would. You do all that time with a nigga, and he come home and start fucking with the next chick. Not me. I done seen it happen to too many bitches. A nigga will never get the chance to do me like that. Ah, ah! Just like Kareem. He thought I was going to do 8 years with him. That nigga must have lost his mind."

Kareem is her ex- boyfriend. They were together for about 5 years. Currently he's in Federal Prison. When he was home, he took care of her to the fullest. He gave her any and everything she asked for.

"You don't feel bad for leaving him like that?" Sincere asks. "You left him at the time he needed you the most."

"Hell no, I don't feel bad! I told him in the very beginning. I told him, I don't do time with no nigga! He still chose to fuck with me. That was on him. I accepted that first phone call, and that's when I told him; I said, remember what I told you in the beginning. He didn't have a clue of what I was talking about. I had to remind him. Then I told him to move on with his life, do him. I told him, ain't no need in worrying if I'm doing me or not, cause I am."

"What did he say?"

"What could he say? He thought I was playing at first until I stopped accepting his calls. Shit, you got the wrong one if you think I'm gone be sitting around waiting for some lame ass nigga!" Mocha shouts as she pulls two plastic cups from the paper bag, along with a small bottle of Tanqueray. She fills both cups with half Tanqueray and half grapefruit juice. She then walks toward Sincere and hands her a cup.

"Here, let's toast," Mocha whispers. They both raise their cups in the air. "To girl's night out!" she yells before tapping Sincere's cup.

CHAPTER 10

Hours Later

The party is off the hook. It's extremely crowded. Everyone is standing shoulder to shoulder, packed in like sardines. Thick clouds of weed smoke fill the air. A person can get high just by being in the room.

The spacious loft is decorated beautifully. It's located on Park Avenue in Manhattan, New York. It belongs to the C.E.O. of the record label. Sincere is overwhelmed, but she's trying to play it cool. So many big-name stars are in here that she can't believe it. She has only seen these people on television so to stand here face to face with them is like a dream come true. People from all the big labels are here: Rocafella Records, Murder Inc., Bad Boy, and Rough Riders.

This is unusual for Sincere, but it's an ordinary night for Mocha. She knows just about everybody in the spot. She stands there nonchalantly as everyone makes their way over to greet her as if *she's* the star.

Mocha is a groupie, but she's what you call a seasoned groupie. She's nothing like the rest of the girls at the party. Those girls are wearing close to nothing. They might as well be naked the way they're exposing all their body parts. They're allowing these dudes to do whatever they choose to do to them.

The bathroom is the VIP room. The traffic flows in and out of there. Every 20 minutes, a new girl escorts three or four dudes in there. The girls walk out looking whipped after degrading themselves and allowing three men to take turns abusing her body. These young girls will do anything just to be down.

They're really balling in here. Bottles of Cristal are

being passed around like cocktails. Mocha has had at least ten bottles sent to her from different people.

Everyone is partying to the max, and the dance floor is jumping. D.J. Funk Master Flex is playing all the hot joints.

The corner of the loft is just as packed as the dance floor. At least 50 dudes are crowded around a 60-inch plasma TV screen. They're playing Play Station's Madden. They're gambling big money, starting at $5,000 a game.

Mocha's favorite song comes on. Her little rap friend Sinister just happens to walk toward her right on time. She grabs hold of his hand and drags him to the dance floor, leaving Sincere alone, leaning against the bar.

She doesn't stand there alone for long though. Before Mocha even hits the dance floor, a visitor approaches Sincere.

"Oh, boy," she thinks to herself. This is the reason she didn't want to come in the first place. The last thing she wants to deal with is a bunch of fronting ass niggas, all in her face lying the entire night. She has rejected at least 20 dudes already. She tries not to be rude, but some of them are so persistent. She has taken a total of ten numbers, although she doesn't plan to use any of them. She just took them to avoid trouble. She knows how rude young guys can get. They're rich, and they think every woman is supposed to fall at their feet. She's afraid if she rejects them they might try to embarrass her, and she hates to be put on the spot. She has already seen three girls get drinks poured in their faces.

"How you doing, lady?" he whispers.

Sincere looks straight ahead at Mocha, acting as if she didn't hear him. She's hoping that he catches the hint that she doesn't want to be bothered and just walks away.

"Excuse me," he whispers.

Please, Sincere thinks to herself.

"Excuse me," he repeats.

"Yes," she replies with an aggravated tone, while looking him directly in the eyes.

He extends his hand for a handshake. "Hello, my name is Reggie. And yours?"

"Jamie," she replies while returning the handshake. Jamie is the alias that she's been using all night.

She's slightly impressed by his approach. She's heard all kinds of corny lines tonight, but he's the first one to approach her with a basic handshake. Besides that, he's about the best-looking dude she has encountered, too. He's a little square looking but the most handsome one by far. He's extremely light complexioned with red, wavy hair. He appears to be a few years younger than she is, and stands about 6 feet even with a medium build.

He looks so out of place in here. He's about the plainest-looking guy in the place. He looks quite average. He's wearing an ordinary-looking velour sweat suit, with brand new, blue and white Nikes to match. He's not wearing any jewelry -not even a watch.

"Jamie, how you doing?"

"Good," she replies with a frustrated tone.

"You wanna dance?" he asks.

"Nah, I don't dance."

"How about a drink then?"

"Nah, I don't drink either."

"Well, how about a little conversation? Oh, let me guess. You don't talk either, huh?" he asks with a clever-looking smile on his face.

She finally cracks a smile. She takes notice of his unusual-colored eyes. She has never seen a black man with baby blue eyes. She wonders if they're real.

"Are you married?" he asks.

"Not yet."

"Good, I'm just in time!"

Please, she thinks to herself. Even if she were single and looking, he wouldn't be a candidate. Red niggas are a turn-off to her. For some strange reason, she could never get along with light-skinned guys. Maybe it's the fact that the majority of them think they're prettier than their women.

She smiles. "Nah, you're already too late."

"You sure?"

"I'm positive."

"So you mean to tell me there's no way I can step in between that?"

"Correct," she whispers with a cute little grin.

"I don't think it's too late. You don't even have a ring yet. If he cared that much, he would have given you a ring already. Shit, if you were with me, I would have branded you already!"

"I got a ring," she shouts as she lifts her left hand up to expose the two-karat, princess- cut stone Suave bought for her birthday a few years ago.

"Let me see," he asks while grabbing hold of her hand. He slowly flips her hand over to examine the ring. "That's cute," he says sarcastically.

Sincere starts to blush.

"Is your boyfriend a Jew?"

"Huh?" she asks, without a clue of what he's talking about.

"Is he Jewish?"

"No, why do you ask that?"

"Nothing, no reason," he says while chuckling.

"Nah, tell me why you asked that," she insists.

"Nah, only a stingy man would buy such a stife ring."

Stife, she thinks to herself. He just fucked up now. She's pissed. He just hurt her feelings. "Stife, what you mean by stife?"

"Nah, I'm only kidding. Don't take me serious."

"What do you mean, stife? This is a two-karat stone."

"Shh, don't scream that too loud. People are listening," he clowns.

He's really pissing her off now. Her face is red from

embarrassment.

"You got some nerve. You ain't wearing not even a half a karat, and you trying to play me. Anyway, I'm content, and that's all that matters."

"Some people are just so easy to please," he mumbles.

Sincere is hot now. She has had just about enough of his slick mouth. She's about to let him have it when his phone rings and interrupts her.

"Hold on," he screams to the person on the other end of the phone. He then calls the waitress over to him. "Listen, get a bottle of Chrissy for my friend right here," he whispers.

As the waitress is walking away, he looks Sincere dead in the eyes. "Don't lose that thought. I'll be right back. We'll pick up where we left off."

Sincere stands there pissed off. She can't wait for him to get back so she can let him have it. She plans to make him feel so small. She's rehearsing in her head what she's going to say to him. The nerve of him trying to belittle her! He's probably the brokest one at the party, and he's talking to her like that. Suave warned her about dudes like him. He's probably about to spend his whole paycheck on the bottle of champagne just to impress her.

Just as the waitress is coming back, Sincere spots him coming toward her. She really doesn't want the champagne, but she's going to crack it open just to call his bluff. Her intentions are to crack it open and spill it purposely. She wants to see his broke ass face when he watches his last $400 spill on the floor.

The waitress pours two glasses for them and sets the bottle on the countertop.

He takes a long sip. "Now, where were we? I think you were about to curse me out. Go ahead, fire away," he says before following up with a big smile.

As Sincere turns her glass up to drink from it, her elbow accidentally or intentionally knocks over the bottle. "Oops!"

she shouts. "I'm so sorry," she lies. Suddenly, she's not mad anymore. She stands the empty bottle up and pats the counter dry with her napkin. "I'm so sorry," she repeats.

"Don't worry about it," he says, as he looks in the direction of the waiter who is walking toward them.

Now, she thinks to herself. That should keep him quiet. To her surprise, he nods at the waiter and orders another bottle.

The song stops playing. Mocha and Sinister are making their way back over.

Reggie immediately grabs two more glasses for Mocha and Sinister. As he's pouring, someone calls him from across the room. "God damn!" he shouts, as if he's tired of being bothered. He eases away from the bar. As he gets halfway across the room, he turns around and calls Sinister. They meet at the center of the room before disappearing into the crowd of people.

"Girl, you done hit the jackpot," Mocha shouts.

"Jackpot? What are you talking about?" Sincere questions.

"You don't know who that is?"

"No, who?" Sincere asks.

"Girl, that's Reggie Red!" Mocha replies.

"Who the hell is Reggie Red?"

"Reggie Red is the CEO of Friend or Foe Entertainment and the owner of this loft we're in. That nigga rich!"

"And?" Sincere asks while trying to act as nonchalant as she can. Now she understands his cocky attitude. She feels silly now because of the way she was bragging to him about her little two-karat stone. She truly didn't realize who she was talking to.

"Girl, that nigga paid up. He lives here in New York, and he has a big ass house in Cali. That's where he spends most of his time. Most of his artists are out there. If you play your cards right, half of all that can be yours!"

"Hello, Mocha! I have a man. Did you forget?"

"Girl, there you go with that shit again. Don't let this one go down the drain. If you do, I'm done with your ass."

"Girl, please!" Sincere replies.

"See, I always told you, you can have any nigga you want. Ain't that something? I got the worker and you got the boss!"

"I ain't got shit. I have a man!"

"I normally don't deal with the help. Usually, if I can't have the top dog, then I don't want nothing. But he alright though; I just gotta work with him. Wait till you see him about a year from now after I step up his game. You won't even know he's the same person."

They laugh, but Mocha is serious. She really believes she can make a man be who she wants him to be. She knows how to use the power of the PUSSY.

After sipping the champagne, Sincere starts to feel a little groovy and begins to loosen up. She finally makes her way to the dance floor where she and Mocha dance for an hour straight.

The party is just about over. Mocha and Sincere are the last two on the dance floor. They're both good and drunk now. They look around, and to their surprise they see that not only is the dance floor empty, but the entire loft has emptied out -all except Reggie Red and Sinister. They're sitting in front of the television playing the video game.

"Girl, it's time to go," says Sincere. "Let's get on home."

The girls walk over to the corner. The fellas are so caught up in the game that they have not noticed the girls standing there.

Mocha bends down, wraps her arms around Sinister's neck, and whispers in his ear. He pauses the game immediately.

"Hold up. Why you leaving?"

"We gotta go."

"Come on Mocha, hold up," he begs. "Hold up, God!" he says while getting up. He grabs Mocha by the hand and pulls her about ten feet away, leaving Sincere and Reggie alone.

"So did you enjoy yourself?" Reggie asks.

"It was a party," Sincere snaps.

"Just a regular party, huh?"

"Yeah, just a regular party," she claims. She's lying through her teeth. She has never had that much fun in her life. She feels so guilty, knowing she had so much fun while Suave is cooped up in somebody's tight jail cell. She hopes like hell that he never gets wind of this.

Mocha steps back over. "Sincere, let's just cool out here for the night," she suggests.

"Girl, you crazy! For the night? You have lost your mind! I'm going home, and you are too. We came together, and we leaving together."

"Come on," she whispers as she sneakily winks her eye at Sincere.

"Hell, no!" she shouts before Mocha jolts her by the arm. She whispers in her ear. "Girl, all that drinking and dancing got me horny as hell. Please stay long enough for me to get a little quickie in. Please?" she begs.

"Mocha, I gotta go home."

"Jamie, it's already 4 in the morning. The sun will be up in another two hours. You might as well squat up. It's too late to be out there driving back to Jersey. And ya'll drunk."

Jamie? Sincere almost forgot the alias she used on him. She winks at Mocha, so she doesn't give her away. She's afraid to tell him her real name. She knows how niggas talk. She doesn't know who he might know. All she would need is for someone to tell Suave she was at this party.

"I'm not staying here. I'm going home."

"Please," Mocha whispers, while making a begging gesture with her hands.

Reggie and Sinister walk over to the stereo system, and Mocha continues to beg Sincere.

"Please?"

"No, ah ah. If I stay here, he's going to expect something."

"Oh no, he ain't, girl. I already told him you ain't like that. As soon as the sun comes up, we out. I promise."

Sincere debates with herself.

"Please," Mocha interrupts.

Sincere hates to spoil her fun. Mocha always calls her a party pooper.

"Alright, but as soon as it gets light, we gotta go. And you better not leave me and him by ourselves."

"Oh, I won't. Thanks, Mommy," Mocha shouts before giving Sincere a tight hug.

The fellas are on their way back over. Sinister is holding a bottle of red wine, and Reggie is carrying a tray full of raw clams, crab legs, cocktail shrimp, and lobster tails.

"Oh, ah ah! Hell no," Sincere yells. "Aphrodisiacs, wine, and slow music? I know what ya'll thinking!"

"Thinking about what?" Reggie innocently asks.

"You know what I'm talking about. I ain't one of them little groupie chicks. You can forget that."

"Forget what? What are you talking about? Listen Ma, I don't want nothing from you but a little conversation. That's it. That's my word! Even if you wanted to give me some, I wouldn't take it."

"Oh, you don't ever have to worry about that. I ain't never gonna want to give you nothing." He has pissed her off again.

"Take it easy, lady. I'm only bugging. Just cool out till the sun come up and your liquor wears off. After that you can go on about your way, alright? I would feel fucked up if something happen to ya'll out there after leaving my spot, feel me? It would be on my conscience my whole life."

Mocha and Sinister sneak off to the far end of the room and disappear behind the partition that separates the two rooms.

Sincere hesitantly plops onto the oversized leather bean bag, which sits in the corner. Reggie sips on the wine and slurps the raw clams. He eats a dozen of them before he decides to offer her some. Together they demolish the entire tray of seafood and gulp up half the bottle of wine.

An hour passes before they realize it. For the past 30 minutes, Reggie has been selling himself to her and telling her all the reasons she should consider giving him a chance to prove to her that he's a good man. He brags on and on about how happy he can make her.

He grabs a pen and a pad from the table. He scribbles three stick figures on the paper.

"This is me, this is you, and this is... what's your boyfriend's name?" he asks.

"Why," she asks quickly. She'll never tell that. She's determined not to leave a trace. Once she walks out of this door, that's it. They'll never see or hear from each other ever again. She can't allow this night to haunt her relationship with Suave. She would hate to live in fear, wondering whether Suave will find out one day.

"Never mind. This is me, this is you, and this is homeboy. Look at the paper," he says as he extends his hand to pass her the pad. "I'll give you $1,000 right now if you circle the character that doesn't belong in our picture."

Sincere smiles bashfully before circling the character that represents him.

"Wrong!" he shouts. "I gave you a clue, and you still got it wrong. I said *our* picture. Let's try this again."

He snatches the pen and the pad and scribbles the exact same picture all over again. He then passes it to her. She snatches it and slams it to the floor.

"Stop it, Reggie," she giggles. "I could never forget about him. I love him more than life itself."

"Oh, I'm not trying to make you forget about him. I would never do that. I just want you to think of me as much as you think of him."

She's speechless. Sincere must admit, Reggie's rather smooth. His persistence really flatters her.

Suddenly, a loud bumping sound interrupts her thoughts. It's the sound of the headboard crashing into the wall.

They both look toward the back where Mocha and her friend are. They can see Mocha's naked silhouette on the wall. She's straddled over him, riding like a cowgirl. She's carrying on as if she has forgotten that they're in the next room. She wasn't lying when she told Sincere she was horny.

Now Sincere feels very uncomfortable. She's trying to act like the noise doesn't exist, but it's hard. Mocha's moaning is echoing throughout the apartment.

Reggie laughs as he notices how uncomfortable the situation is making Sincere. The session lasts for about ten minutes before the noise stops.

Reggie goes to the bathroom and starts to run the water for his shower.

Sincere lays her head back and vibes to the music. Two minutes later, she falls sound asleep.

Three Hours Later

Sincere wakes up to a foreign room. The liquor has worn off. It takes her a few seconds to realize where she is.

Right now, she has a terrible headache. Her hangover has kicked in. Reggie is layed out across the carpet, knocked out.

Sincere can faintly hear Mocha and Sinister going at it again. Now she knows why men go so crazy for Mocha. She's like a *fucking machine*.

Sincere has a different perception about Reggie after talking to him. Not one time did he attempt to touch her or even suggest sex. That's hard to believe. He behaved like the perfect gentleman.

She looks at the clock. It reads 10 o' clock. Oh shit, she thinks to herself. She has to be at work in two hours.

She nudges Reggie with her feet until he wakes up groggy eyed.

"Huh?"

"I gotta go. Go tell Mocha it's time to leave."

Mocha hears her and steps out of the room. She's wearing a sheer, see - through bra and panty set. All her goods are exposed. There's no shame in her game. She stands there confidently as if Reggie isn't even in there. He gives her one good stare up and down before turning away and walking to the bathroom. Sincere and Mocha can't help but notice the bulge in his pants from his morning hard-on. He tries to pull his shirt over to conceal it, but it's already too late.

"Come on girl, let's go. I gotta get to work."

"Oh, I forgot today is a work day. You know me; it's all the same for me. Friday is just like Monday to me."

Sincere stands up and tries to press the wrinkles out of her clothes, while Mocha disappears into the back room.

Ten minutes later, all three of them reappear. Sinister rushes into the bathroom, half asleep.

"At least let me feed ya'll. I can't let ya'll leave like that. That would make me a poor host. Let's go out and get some breakfast."

"Boy, I gotta be at work by noon."

"Call in sick. I'll pay you for the day. What you make, $75 or $80 a day?"

"$75 or $80 a day! Try $300 a day! I keep telling you, I ain't one of your little chicken - head groupies."

"Three hundred dollars a day? Alright, take the week off. I got you." He smiles from ear to ear. "Nah, for real though. Let's get a bite to eat, alright?"

"Come on Sincere, call in sick. You can take one day off.

It ain't gone hurt you. You been working like a slave. That's all you do is work, work, work. You deserve a day off."

That's one thing Sincere hates about Mocha. Whenever one of her boyfriends has a friend that wants Sincere, Mocha tries her best to get them together. She tries to use Sincere to make them tighter. She'll agree with damn near everything he says just to stay on his good side.

"Girl, you pressing your luck. I knew I shouldn't have came here with you. You are a bad influence. You turn a party into a vacation." Sincere weighs her options. She really does deserve a rest from work. She's been working so hard ever since Suave went away. She uses work to keep her mind off of him. "I can't go nowhere with these wrinkled ass clothes on. Look at me, I look a mess."

"Look at all of us," Reggie says. "You ain't by yourself."

Sinister hurries out of the bathroom. "Mocha, I'm gone. Yo Red, Peace!"

"Peace, God," Reggie replies.

"Alright, hit me later," Mocha blurts out.

"He's not going with us?" Sincere asks.

"Nah, he has a studio session in 15 minutes," Mocha replies.

"Where are we going?" Sincere questions.

"There's a nice little restaurant around the corner on Fifth Avenue. We can go there," Reggie suggests.

It takes Mocha and Sincere approximately 35 minutes to shower up and prepare themselves. Once they're done, they catch the elevator downstairs. Reggie told them he would be waiting for them in front of the building.

Once they get outside, they get the shock of a lifetime. They knew he would be in front of the building, but they didn't expect him to be sitting out there in a Bentley.

It's beautiful. It's black with a snow-white interior. It's the four-door Bentley Arnage. Sincere is not too good with recognizing cars, but she knows this one pretty well because it's Suave's dream car. He loves it. He saves any magazine that has that particular car featured in it.

They hop in the car hesitantly. Sincere forces Mocha to sit in the front seat. She won't dare ride in the front seat and risk someone seeing her. Suave would be crushed. He promised her he was going to give her the pleasure of riding in a Bentley. It would break his heart to know that another man gave her that pleasure first.

Sincere sinks into the butter-soft leather. The car is detailed beautifully. The seats are piped out with black trim. The floor mats are made from thick, chinchilla-fur. They have his company logo imprinted on them, and the steering wheel also has the logo in the center of it. The dashboard and the doors have an onyx finish trimmed with platinum.

He turns on the CD player. The sound of "I love the Dough" by Jay Z and Biggie blares through the speakers.

He pulls off aggressively. The car rides so smoothly that they can barely feel it moving.

Reggie makes a left followed by a quick right. He then pulls directly in front of Saks Fifth Avenue. He reaches in his pocket and pulls out a hefty knot of $100 bills. He peels 20 bills from his stack and passes them over to Mocha.

"Mo, ya'll go get something to wear. I know ya'll ain't gone feel comfortable with those clothes on. Force her to buy something, too."

"I'm not taking money from you," says Sincere.

"You ain't taking it from me. Mo giving it to you!" he shouts with a devilish smile on his face.

Mocha hurries out of the car before he changes his mind. Sincere drags way behind.

Reggie waits out front for an hour as Mocha goes on a mini shopping spree. She doesn't stop until she has spent the entire $2,000 on them. Out of $2,000, Mocha only managed to get jeans, shoes, shades, and underwear for the two of them.

While they were shopping, Mocha continuously begged Sincere to give Reggie a chance. For some strange reason, Sincere is starting to believe that Reggie and Mocha put this whole ordeal together.

After changing clothes in the dressing room, they hop in the car and Reggie pulls off. They have no clue where his destination is. He jumps on the Triborough Bridge and takes that to the Grand Central Parkway.

Sincere watches attentively as he exits the Van Wyck Expressway. Reggie Red cruises the grounds of the JFK Airport and parks in the parking lot.

"Where are we going?" Sincere asks.

"To lunch, being that we missed breakfast," he replies.

They follow close behind him as he walks through the revolving doors of Continental Airlines. He storms to the counter and orders three first class tickets.

They still don't have a clue where he's taking them.

"Ah, ah, you gone tell me where you taking me," Sincere shouts.

"I already told you, to lunch."

"Where?"

"At the restaurant," he replies sarcastically.

Fifteen minutes later, they're at the ramp stepping into the plane. Sincere is now second-guessing the entire situation, but it's too late. The plane is departing.

90 Minutes Later

Before they can even get comfortable, the plane begins to land. That was the shortest flight Sincere has ever been on.

As they step out of the airport, they realize that they're in Washington, D.C.

Reggie flags down a cab and opens the door for them to get in. They ride for a few minutes before pulling up to the *1789*

Restaurant.

Sincere can't believe he flew them all the way there just to eat lunch. She's impressed by his style and his character.

Immediately after eating, they jump right back on the plane and head back to New York.

As Sincere is driving back to Jersey, her mind plays all kinds of tricks on her. She hasn't had that much fun in a long time. She has never met a dude like Reggie. She can't believe how much trouble he went through just for a lunch. In fact, he paid close to $5,000 for a lunch date. She knows that all of that could have been part of his game -but then again, maybe not. That may just as well be his everyday life. For a second, she wonders what it would be like to be with someone like him. She feels guilty even thinking like that, but she's sure it's her loneliness causing those thoughts. She wouldn't trade Suave for the world. Besides, a guy like Reggie would be nothing but a headache. She's sure he has girls all over the world.

He demanded she take his number, even after she told him she would never call.

Mocha told her to play him for what he's worth, but Sincere isn't that kind of girl. Or, is she?

CHAPTER 11

Thirty Days Later/March 2002

Today is Suave's first day out of lock-up. The month he spent out of population was rough on him. The first week was torture, but by the second week he had gotten used to being alone. He tried to make the best of the situation. He used the month to undergo a self-bettering process.

For the entire month, all he did was read and think. He passed most of the day away by reading. In the little time he was down there, he read at least ten books. That's something big to him, because when he was home he never even thought about reading a book. He doesn't read the newspaper, magazines, or anything. He really fell in love with two books. They're by some new writer. The titles are *No Exit* and *Block Party*. The reason he loves them so much is because he can relate to them. Those two books really opened his eyes to the game and made him come to a few conclusions. One of them is that he doesn't want to be a drug dealer for the rest of his life. He hasn't figured out what he's going to do or what he can do to generate the type of cash flow he is accustomed to getting. It's not too late though. He still has 15 more months left before he hits the streets again.

As Suave walks onto the tier the sounds of loud clapping welcome him back. "Yeah! Welcome home!"

Home, Suave says to himself. These guys consider this home. Suave knows he's a long way from home.

After the hugs and handshakes, Suave makes his way to the phone.

"Hello?" Sincere answers.

"Sincere, what's up?"

"Oh, hey."

"What the fuck do you mean, oh, hey?"

"Suave, please don't start! I didn't mean anything by that. I was dozing off."

"Yeah alright."

"Please, not tonight baby. I had a rough day at work."

"You had a rough day? What about me? I had 596 rough days. Or did you forget that?"

"Forget? How the fuck can I forget? You're not in this by yourself. I'm doing this bid with you. Never once have you said thank you for being by your side."

"Thank you? What the fuck do you mean thank you? Are you waiting for me to say thank you? You're not doing me a favor by being by my side. You're supposed to do that. I've held you down for ten motherfucking years."

"Suave, listen. I didn't mean it like that!"

"Thank you." Click! He slams down the phone. He's enraged.

Afterwards, he goes to his cell and does push ups. It's either that or kill somebody in there. He has to find some way to take out his frustrations.

For the rest of the day, he just stays to himself. He doesn't converse with anyone, not even Good Muslim. Over the past couple of months, Good Muslim's lectures are the only thing that has kept him sane.

After coming to his senses and clearing his head some, Suave notices that the tier is quieter than normal today. Usually by this time, Flex and his entourage would be running around causing confusion. Suave hasn't seen him all day. Everyone told him Flex had been real quiet ever since Salaam pimp slapped him. He's been keeping a low profile. He's probably too embarrassed to show his face. They say his business has taken a fall ever since the slapping. Seeing Salaam slap him made everyone realize he isn't that tough after all. He's nothing but a punk hiding behind all those muscles, just like El- Amin said. What he needs to do is go to the wizard and exchange half of those muscles for a heart. He can be compared to the great big elephant in the jungle who is afraid of a little old mouse.

Good Muslim tells Suave that on commissary day, Flex didn't even come out of his cell. Rahiem made a few moves just so the rest of them could eat. Good Muslim says there is no way they can all eat off that little package for the rest of the month. That means a lot of inmates will be starving by the middle of the month.

Suave is so stressed out he can't get a wink of sleep. Earlier today, he acted on emotions with Sincere. Now he regrets it. He knows he never should have reacted like that, but it's the pressure. It's really starting to wear him down. He's ready to go home. It almost feels like he can't take it anymore. Every night he envisions Sincere in bed with another man. He always has those visions, but the past month has been the worst. He has been feeling a terrible vibe, and he doesn't know why. El- Amin always told him to follow his first instincts. He also said, "If you have a gut feeling about something, then nine times out of ten, you're right. The gut doesn't lie."

Suave is about ready to cut the ties with her just so he can have peace of mind.

He falls asleep while debating whether he should or should not cut her off.

CHAPTER 12

The Next Afternoon

Just as Suave is re-reading a stack of letters that Sincere has written over the months, Good Muslim walks in. He has a great big smile on his face. He's just coming from court.

Suave looks up briefly and lowers his eyes back to the letter. In the letter, Sincere reminds him of how much she loves him and how she really misses him. The scent of Ralph Lauren fills the air. The paper is dipped in her favorite perfume. Suave loves it too, because she wears it every day.

"P.S. I love you so much. I can't wait until you come home! Sincerely yours." He reads aloud. She ends all the letters with *Sincerely Yours* with an imprint of her lips plastered to the bottom of the paper in cherry-red lipstick.

Suave lifts the paper to his nose one more time and takes a big sniff before putting it back into the envelope.

"What's up, Beloved?" Good Muslim asks. Beloved is what he calls Suave.

"Not too much," Suave mumbles. "Why are you so happy?"

"Things are looking good for me. My attorney found a lot of loopholes. Looks like I might be giving a lot of this time back."

"Oh, yeah?" Suave questions.

"Yes, Sir!"

Good Muslim has high hopes. Suave hates to crush them, but he doesn't think Good Muslim has a chance. He has a little over ten years in on a double life sentence. Suave never asked him what he did to get all that time. He felt uncomfortable asking him that. He figured one day Good

Muslim would just open up and offer the information.

"Can I ask you a question, Good Muslim?"

"Sure, whatever."

"How do you keep your hopes up like you do, knowing what you're facing?"

Good Muslim pauses for a second.

"Through my faith. God knows best. Whatever God decrees, that's what it will be. If God ordains me to spend the rest of my life here, then this is where I will be. No one will be able to change that. My past is what got me in the jam that I'm in now. I can't change the past. All I can do is prepare for the future."

"But what kind of future will you have if you have to spend the rest of your life behind bars?"

Good Muslim pauses.

"Do you know how many lives I have changed since I've been in here? In the ten years that I've been in here, I've turned a few dozen cold-hearted criminals into righteous Muslims. Thanks to God," he adds. "Some may say they're jailhouse Muslims or they only became Muslims for protection, but whatever the case may be, they're still Muslims. Sure, a lot of people become Muslim in jail -the statistics show you that, but the statistics don't show you that a great percentage of those that become Muslim in jail, once they're released they never return."

Good Muslim has Suave's undivided attention. Suave is looking him directly in the eyes as he speaks. Suave is barely blinking. "I wasn't always a righteous Muslim. As you can see, I ran the streets just like everyone else in here. If it wasn't for prison, maybe I would have never became Muslim. If I never go home, then I'll take it that this is where I'm supposed to be. Maybe this is my calling. Maybe God put me here to change other people's lives."

"And you cool with that?" Suave asks.

"I don't have a choice."

"Good Muslim, do you have a family on the outside? I mean a wife and kids?"

"No, I don't have a wife or kids. The only outside connection to the world that I have is through my attorney. He's been with me from day one. He's a good guy. He's been holding me down the whole bid. Whatever I need, he makes sure I have. He visits me twice a month. He's been doing that for almost 11 years. He says he's going to get me out of here. I take his word for it."

At that moment, Suave realizes that his stress is small compared to Good Muslim's stress, along with that of a number of other inmates. In about 15 months he'll be home doing his thing again, whereas these guys will finish off in here.

After the conversation, Suave decides to call and patch things up with Sincere. Just to think, he actually considered letting her go, whereas brothers like Good Muslim would do anything to have a strong woman by their side.

CHAPTER 13

Six Months Later/September 2002

The other day, Sincere gave Suave heartbreaking news. She told him El- Amin is suffering from kidney failure.

The past six months have been the worst for Suave. On top of the shocking news, Officer Schneider and Officer Jones are making his life a living hell. Anything they can do to get under his skin, they've done it. When another officer assigns him to clean-up detail, they snatch him off the job just so they can limit his movements. They also limit his phone time. They're even holding his mail back from him. He either gets the mail late or he doesn't receive it at all. Sincere sent him a birthday card, and he didn't receive it until two months later. That caused a big argument. Suave thought she had forgotten his birthday. She never receives any of the letters he mails her. The letters never make it out of the mailroom.

The communication gap is really starting to take its toll on their relationship. They only speak to each other about every other day for a minute or so.

The pressure is starting to break Suave. Good Muslim keeps him on point. Besides his workout partners, Good Muslim is the only inmate Suave has constant dealings with —oh, and Flex, who has eased his way into their circle. He tags along with Suave and Good Muslim all day long. Mainly he stays under Good Muslim. Maybe he does that so Good Muslim can save him from Salaam, or maybe he's trying to change his life around. Who knows?

Today, all three of them have visitors. Flex's wife and kids have just arrived. Good Muslim even has a visitor.

Sincere is on her way. She's still standing in the long

line. Suave can see her clearly from where he's sitting.

As he waits impatiently, he glances over the visiting hall. A lot of kids are visiting today because school is about to start back up. Jailhouse fathers, Suave thinks to himself. Suave watches fathers scold their little bad ass sons as if this one day out of the week is going to make a difference in the week to come.

Today is awakening day for Suave. He knows he has to change his life around because he doesn't want to be like these guys, raising their children from prison. His motto is "Prisoners raise future prisoners." He can't imagine being able to hug your little ones only once or twice a week, or being able to communicate with them only through telephones. Children need to see your facial expression when you're talking to them. They need to learn how to look you directly in the eyes when they're talking to you, whether they're wrong or right. That teaches them to stand strong and face the world, no matter what conditions they're facing. Suave learned all of that from Uncle El- Amin. Where was he when he taught Suave all of this? He was in prison.

Right here, right now, Suave promises himself, this is the first and last time he's ever going to prison.

"Beloved!" Good Muslim shouts. Suave turns his head instantly at the sound of Good Muslim's voice. "Come here, I want you to meet somebody."

As Suave walks over to the table, he takes a quick look at the visitor. He's a short guy, wearing a New Jersey Nets basketball jersey with a matching hat, which is turned backwards. He has on big, baggy jeans and Timberland boots. He's also wearing a white-gold Patek Philippe watch.

As Suave approaches them, the visitor stands up and starts collecting his papers from the table, jamming them into a briefcase. This isn't your average briefcase. This briefcase is made of alligator skin, and it's trimmed in ostrich.

"Beloved, this is my attorney." Then he looks at the

attorney and says, "This is Beloved. That's what I call him; everyone else calls him Suave."

Your attorney, Suave thinks to himself. This guy sure does not look like an attorney. He looks like the average street corner nigga.

"You look shocked," says Good Muslim.

Suave smiles. "Nah, it's just, he doesn't look like a lawyer."

The lawyer laughs. "What do I look like, a hustler?" the lawyer asks with a grin on his face.

"Yeah!" Suave shamefully, admits while nodding his head up and down.

They all laugh. The lawyer and Suave shake hands. "Pleased to meet you," says the lawyer.

"Likewise," answers Suave.

"Alright ya'll, I'm outta here," the lawyer shouts.

"Hold up!" Good Muslim interrupts. "Show him the good news before you leave."

The attorney opens the briefcase and pulls a sheet of paper from it. He then hands the paper to Suave. Suave examines it, but he doesn't have a clue what it's about. The paper is full of legal terms. Suave hands back the paper.

"Did you read it?" Good Muslim asks.

"Yeah, but I don't have a clue what I read."

They all laugh. "It states that he'll be eligible for parole in one more year," says the lawyer.

"Yeah?" Suave asks with a surprising tone.

"What did I tell you?" shouts Good Muslim. "I told you he would get me out of here."

"There are a lot of loopholes in his case. It took me a few years, but I finally found an opening to squeeze him through."

Good Muslim is wearing the biggest Kool-Aid smile. Suave has never seen him act like this. He hardly ever smiles; he's always real serious.

Suave is happy for him. Good Muslim is such a nice and

humble guy. Prison is no place for a guy like him to finish his life. Suave can't imagine what he did to land himself in here.

"Alright, E Boogie," the lawyer shouts.

"Abdur Rahman," Good Muslim interrupts sarcastically.

The lawyer smiles. "Okay, okay, Abdur Rahman," he revises. "I have to go. Make sure you call my office on Monday."

"I'll call you bright and early, if God is willing," says Good Muslim. "Tony, thanks for everything."

"Stop thanking me. We're family. Real niggas do real things," the lawyer shouts as he walks toward the exit.

"You got it, Nephew," Good Muslim says sarcastically.

By this time, Sincere is making her way through the entrance. The sweet smell of her perfume beats her to the table. She's wearing the tightest jeans you could ever imagine. As she passes everyone, they're turning their heads to see where the fruitful scent is coming from.

As she approaches the table where Suave is seated, his face begins to distort. As she sits down, the distorted look turns to a look of pure anger.

"What's up, baby?" she asks.

"Don't what's up me," he replies. "I'm starving! What happened to my food package this month?"

"Huh?" she questions with a confused look on her face.

"I don't have shit. I've been living off my cell mate."

"What the hell are you talking about? I sent your motherfucking food package. I don't know what the hell you're talking about!" Sincere is getting frustrated with him. She hardly ever speaks to him with this type of language.

"You sent it?" he asks.

"Yeah, I told you I sent it."

Suave looks dumbfounded. He doesn't understand. He should have received that package weeks ago.

As he sits there trying to figure out what could have happened, Officer Schneider comes walking toward their table.

He walks past slowly. He looks Suave directly in the eyes with a look as cold as stone. The officer mumbles the words *punk motherfucker* under his breath. That's when Suave realizes who is behind the plot of keeping his food package from him. The two dickheads are at it again: Officer Schneider and Officer Jones.

Schneider stands against the wall directly behind Suave's chair. Suave tries to act as if he isn't there. He's doing a good job, but the look on Sincere's face shows that his presence is making her feel uncomfortable.

"Later for him," Suave whispers, trying to take her mind off of the officer.

"Suave, I have something to tell you," she whispers.

"Go ahead."

Sincere hesitates like she is at a loss for words.

"Go ahead, what is it?"

"I don't know how to tell you this," she claims.

Uh oh, she's about to drop the bomb on me, Suave thinks to himself. This is the day he's been dreading -the day when Sincere tells him she can no longer be there for him, the day she tells him she has to move on.

He can't look her in the eyes. His eyes are wandering in every other direction except hers. "What's up," he whispers, as he waits for her to drop the bomb.

She reaches over and grabs hold of his hand. He slowly looks up at her. She stares into his eyes as she firmly squeezes his hand. The anxiety is killing him. It's almost like he's waiting to die. Who is it? Where did she meet him? Is he a co-worker? It must be an old boyfriend. His thoughts are running wild. The suspense is driving him crazy.

"Who is he?" he blurts out unsuspectingly.

"Huh?" she asks.

"Who the fuck is he? Is it an old friend?"

"What are you talking about?" she asks.

"Who is he?"

"He who?" she questions.

"The nigga you leaving me for!"

Suave is getting furious. The stupid look on her face is making him angrier by the second. "Bitch, you better tell me who he is," he mumbles under his breath.

She shakes her head with a confused look on her face. "Bitch?" she asks.

"Yeah, bitch," he whispers.

"Hmphh," she snickers. "I'm not talking about a nigga. What is the matter with you? You're going crazy!" she shouts. "I'm talking about Kilo."

"What about Kilo?"

She pauses for a few seconds. "He's dead," she whispers.

"Dead?" he asks with a high-pitched voice.

"Dead," she replies. "They found his body slumped over the steering wheel of his truck. Someone shot him twice in the head."

Suave sits there motionless. He can't believe what she just told him. This can't be true. Kilo is his best friend in the whole world. They're tighter than brothers. They were inseparable until Kilo caught a case about four years ago. After he made bail, he skipped town to Virginia, where he opened up shop. He was down there making a killing. He and Suave rarely saw each other. He would come up once a month, only to re-up. He would come up and get enough work to last him the month.

In Virginia, Kilo was the connection. He sold birds to those country boys for close to double what you could get for them up north. Only Suave knows exactly how many kilos he went through a month.

Suave can't believe what he's hearing. He refuses to accept this as the truth. This is not the way it's supposed to go, he thinks to himself. Kilo wasn't supposed to go out like that. He was supposed to grow old and fat. "Dead?" he repeats.

"Yeah, dead," she whispers.

"When?"

"A couple of days ago," she replies.

This is definitely terrible news. This news is even worse than the shocking news of El-Amin being sick. Suave feels helpless. There's nothing he can do from the inside.

He pictures Kilo slumped over the steering wheel. It's almost like his life just stopped. This has definitely been the worst months of his life.

One week before Suave turned himself in, him and Kilo re-united on the money tip. Suave matched Kilo's $100,000. Kilo promised him if he did so, he would juggle the money until Suave came home. Suave was depending on that money. He was 100 percent sure he could trust Kilo to hold it for him.

For the duration of the visit, Suave was not there mentally. He just sat there dazing off into space, reminiscing about the good times they shared. Kilo died with no kids, no one to carry on his name. Kilo always told Suave that he was waiting for the right woman. He died still seeking that woman. Kilo was in Virginia running from a few years. Those couple of years cost him his life.

Suave was so deep in thought that Officer Schneider's presence didn't even bother him.

It's not even the money that has him stressing. All the money in the world couldn't replace the bond they had.

When the visit was over Suave didn't kiss Sincere. He just stepped away from the table with a blank look on his face. He can't believe it; his brother from another mother is dead. The fact that he'll never see Kilo's face in the physical form ever again is hard for him to digest.

CHAPTER 14

Two Months Later

Two months have slowly dragged by. For Suave, the two months felt like two years. Things have been rough for him. He still hasn't gotten over the fact that Kilo is dead.

Officer Schneider and Officer Jones have stepped their game all the way up and have managed to make Suave's stay a nightmare. Things got so bad that Suave had to go to Internal Affairs. He didn't report the officers, but he did ask them to switch him to another side. He told them he feared getting into trouble with some officers if he remained on that side. They switched him like he requested. Now the only time he has to deal with them is in the visiting hall. He felt like a sucker asking to be moved, but there was nothing he could do. Niggas run the streets, but corrections officers run the jails. They can make your stay a comfortable one, or they can make it a living hell.

He barely knows anyone on this side, but that's better for him. Now he can just do his time in peace. This is the federal side. It's much easier to do your time over here than on the regular state side. Over here the atmosphere is different. There are no car thieves or purse-snatchers. It's mainly white-collar criminals, or big willy- type dudes. Basically, whatever anyone on this side was doing, they were doing it big, whether it was fraudulent checks or boatloads of cocaine.

By chance, Suave and his cell mate are already familiar with each other. They don't know each other personally, but they were introduced to each other a few years ago through a mutual friend.

Suave hasn't received a letter from Sincere in more than

a month, and with her working so hard, he only speaks to her about three times a week. The last time he spoke to her, she told him Uncle El- Amin wasn't doing too well.

No one from the projects pays Sincere anymore. With El- Amin being sickly, no one is enforcing the issue. As the saying goes: "Punks only respect pressure." Sincere doesn't even bother to go through there anymore.

Suave is going through a great deal of depression. Up until two weeks ago, he hadn't even left his cell. His cell mate finally persuaded him to go out for some air. They went to the gym, but Suave didn't go anywhere near the pull-up bar. He just stood around the boxing ring watching his cell mate spar another inmate. Suave has always had a love for boxing.

After about two weeks of watching, Suave decided to join in. To everyone's surprise Suave looked like he had been boxing all his life; he's a natural. When he's in that ring he moves around like a seasoned professional. No one can believe that he has never boxed before.

Only a few inmates can beat him. The rest of them just take the ass beatings he gives them. He pounds them damn near to death, taking out all his frustrations on their bodies.

After a few days, everyone stopped coming to the corner of the gym where the ring is. They fear being called out and having to get in the ring with him. They all know he's a beast with more than two years of stress built up inside him.

CHAPTER 15

One Month Later/December 2002

"Oooh, right there, right there!"

It's 2 in the morning. The place is Suave and Sincere's bedroom.

"Ungh yes, yes!" That's Sincere, but that isn't Suave. How could it be Suave? He's still incarcerated. He has another six months to do before he gets released.

"You like that?"

"Yes, right there," Sincere shouts.

"You want me to go harder?" he asks.

"Yes, harder!" she answers.

He begins to pound on her. "Like that?"

"Yes, like that."

He continues to wail on her.

"I'm about to come!" she cries.

Her entire body trembles as he starts pumping faster. "Stop, stop, don't move," she whispers.

"Aghh," they sigh in harmony.

He immediately falls asleep, while Sincere drags herself to the bathroom to wash up.

After cleaning herself up, she makes her way back to the bedroom. As she's walking through the hallway, she picks up her blouse. A couple of steps later, she bends over to pick up her jeans. As she gets to the bed, she bends over to pick up her panties and her bra. She folds everything up and places it on the rocking chair, which is sitting next to the bed. She then reaches over to the nightstand and grabs the empty bottle of champagne, along with the two empty cups. She discards them into the wastebasket.

They had been sipping on champagne and listening to slow music ever since 8 o' clock. By 10:30, Sincere was drunk out of her mind, but she still continued to sip. By 11:45, Sincere was laying belly-up screaming for mercy as he fulfilled her needs and made her feel like the woman she had almost forgotten she was. Up until then, she was sexually frustrated. Thirty months without sex had literally driven her crazy.

Finally, she leans over and picks up his pants from the floor. She folds them neatly. As she picks up his shirt, something falls out of the front pocket. She bends over quickly and grabs hold of it. She neatly pins the badge back onto the left pocket.

Yes, the badge. The badge has the letters JONES printed on it. It's Officer Jones. Sincere is sleeping with the enemy. Not only did she sleep with him, she sexed him crazily.

CHAPTER 16

Two Months Later

Only four more months to go and Suave will be going home.

As Sincere lines up with the other visitors, her heart begins to skip beats. The guilt is killing her. Officer Jones and three other officers are huddling in the corner. She feels like she's the main topic of their little conversation.

As she slowly advances in the line, Officer Schneider begins to walk toward her. The girl who stands two people ahead of Sincere stops him to question him about something. He answers quickly and continues to walk toward Sincere.

As he approaches her, he has his big blue eyes glued to her breasts. Due to the chill in the building, Sincere's nipples are protruding through her tight blouse. She looks at him in disgust as he looks at them shamelessly. His eyes show pure lust.

He finally passes her. When he gets behind her, he backs up against the wall and begins to watch her perversely. Sincere feels so uncomfortable, it's almost like he's undressing her with his eyes. He doesn't have to use too much of his imagination, because her skintight mini-skirt shows it all. She has the prettiest long legs. Her diamond fluttered ankle bracelet wraps tightly around her ankle.

As she's standing there, her mind begins to wander. Has D'andre (Officer Jones) told Officer Shneider about their sexual encounter? Does he know the noises she makes in bed? The thought of that makes her feel nude before him.

As she steps through the corridor, Suave's face is the first face she spots. Oh my God, she thinks to herself. Standing right behind Suave, already posting up, is D'andre.

Sincere hesitantly approaches the table where Suave is sitting. Suave is so happy to see her that he jumps up instantly.

The scent of her perfume reaches the table before she does. She tries not to look at D'andre. She looks Suave in the eyes. She can feel D'andre watching her the whole time.

Out of the corner of her eye, she can see him looking at her with a look of arrogance.

Suave opens his arms wide, hoping for a hug, but Sincere only grabs hold of both of his hands and swings them lightly. Suave steps closer to her. He's hoping for a kiss, but instead she sits down quickly. D'andre hasn't taken his eyes off of them yet.

"Damn, no kiss?" he asks as he slowly sits down.

Sincere cracks a half a smile and pushes her body forward. Suave quickly rises up and meets her halfway.

Sincere peeks from the corner of her eye. She can see D'andre slowly shaking his head in disgust.

"What's up, baby?" Suave asks.

"Nothing much," she whispers. She's not looking Suave in his eyes. She has her eyes fixed on the center of the table. She feels so terrible that she can't face him. Actually, she feels like a slut. She wishes she could take back that night. She doesn't know why she betrayed him like that. He has never given her a reason to cheat on him. He's such a good man. She hadn't planned on having sex with D'andre; she was only looking for a little conversation, but the champagne and her raging hormones were a terrible mix.

She knows she was dead wrong for sleeping with him, but she got weak. He caught her at the time in her life when she was most vulnerable. Her desire to be touched and loved made her weak. His persistence reeled her in. At every visit, he had a slick remark for her. His attractiveness made it worse. Although Suave is a brown-skinned brother, Sincere has always been a sucker for a chocolate-colored man.

Chocolate, D'andre is. His ebony skin glistens flawlessly. He doesn't have a scratch or a razor bump anywhere. Besides his thick mustache, he's clean-shaven. He has thick, dark eyebrows and jet-black curly hair. His big curls overlap his skin-tight fade. Women love his smile. His big pearly whites are so perfect they look unreal. His eyes are what top off the picture. Black as he is, he has hazel brown eyes that makes him look demonic. Even though he's about six inches too short to be a model, it's still hard for any woman to resist him. He only stands 5 feet 6 inches tall, but his broad shoulders make up for the height disadvantage. Being that he's so athletically inclined, his body is put together perfectly. He has even won a few bodybuilding competitions.

"So you're going to keep that hair, huh?" she asks.

"I told you I'm not letting these niggas cut my hair," he replies. "Besides, I only got a few more months left."

Sincere hates Suave's new look. His good hair has converted into short dreadlocks, and his thick, raggedy beard makes him look so unattractive to her. The beard she could probably deal with, but his hair she despises. She's also a sucker for a nigga with a good grade of hair.

Sincere notices that Suave has put on a few extra pounds. He's no longer her tall, slinky baby. His tight, thermal, long-john shirt is glued to him, especially across his shoulders. The humps on his shoulders are so big, they almost make him look deformed. His chest looks as if it's going to bust through his shirt any minute.

He catches her admiring his physique. He teases her by arrogantly making his chest bounce. He smiles devilishly as he does so.

"I might have to bring you one of my bras the next time I come," she whispers.

He blushes.

Suave slowly puts his right hand underneath the table while holding her hand with his left. He gently squeezes her knee. He then begins to stroke her knee with the tip of his finger. He slowly drags his finger from her knee up her inner thigh. Her skin is so soft and smooth. She tries to resist him by closing her legs tightly. He pries them open by applying a little pressure with his backhand. The smooth feeling of silk greets his hand as he encounters her crotch area. He feels the tension as he slowly pets her love box. Finally, she gives in. She slowly spreads her legs wide open and slouches down in her chair. Suave applies more pressure as he massages her. He knows it's getting to her because he can feel the moisture seeping through her silky panties. He clumsily fumbles for the elastic, which is tightly clamped around her juicy thighs. After locating it, he jams his finger in between the elastic and her leg. Her panties are now soaked. After teasing her lips with strokes that are as light as a feather, he finally works his way to the top. Her love button is standing up attentively. At the touch of his fingertip, she opens her legs even wider. With his index finger, he manages to slide her panties to the side a little more. While holding her panties with one finger, he slides the tip of his middle finger inside her. As he strokes her love button with his thumb, he slides his index finger deeper inside her. Her insides are so creamy. He slowly fingers her in and out. He's driving her insane.

She then puts her hand under the table and reaches for his tool. It only takes her seconds to locate it. She grabs hold of the rock-hard cannon and begins to grope it. He fingers her faster, and she gropes him faster. Suddenly, her legs begin to tremble. Suave feels the cream drip down his finger.

Through all of the commotion, Officer Dick Head has not noticed anything.

Suave smiles at Sincere as he lifts his hand from underneath the table. Her cheeks are blushed from embarrassment.

He slyly lifts his finger up to his nose and takes a big sniff. He truly misses her aroma. He slowly licks her juices

98

from his finger while looking directly in her eyes.

He's so heated, he wishes he hadn't started fondling her. All he did was tease himself.

The visiting hall becomes extremely quiet as Suave's cell mate makes his grand appearance. The tall young man struts gracefully through the hall like a model walks the runway.

"Come here!" Suave calls to him as he approaches. "I want you to meet my fiancée!" he shouts. "Sincere, that's my bunkie," he whispers.

He finally gets to the table. There he stands wearing a tight-fitted thermal shirt, beige khakis, and state-issued boots.

Sincere's eyes almost look up to the heavens as she looks at him. She didn't lock eyes with him. She knows that's a no no to lock eyes with anyone while she's around Suave. He'll kill her. He's always told her that's a form of lust, and some cats could misjudge it and think that she wants them.

This dude is about 6 feet 8 inches tall, and he's well proportioned. The way his thermal shirt fits him makes Suave's look like it's too big. The shirt is stretched to the maximum. You can see that the stitching of the seams is about to bust loose. The sleeves of the shirt only come to the middle of his forearm. The veins in his forearm are protruding through his skin because the tight elastic is cutting off his circulation.

"Yo, this is my fiancée."

"Hello," says Sincere.

"How are you?" he asks. "I've heard so much about you. It's a pleasure to finally meet you."

"Likewise," she replies.

"Let me get on over to my people," he says, while pointing to a table about ten feet away. At the table sits an old Philippine-looking woman and a beautiful Chinese woman. Suave's cell mate had already told him that his mother is Philippine. The Chinese girl is his lady. She is definitely as beautiful as he described her.

"They came all the way from down south just to see me.

Alright Sincere, see you later!"

"Alright, later," she mumbles.

Officer Jones has a cheesy grin on his face while watching Suave's bunkie walk away. "Mayor," he shouts.

"What up, Jones? What are you doing over here? I told you about bothering my man."

"I ain't bothering him. I'm just doing my job," Jones replies.

"Alright, Jones!"

"Alright, Mayor!"

Suave's cell mate has all the officers on lock. They move at his command. Suave told him why he had to leave the other side. He then sent word to Jones through another officer telling him to back off of Suave. Suave hasn't had a problem with him ever since. The most he'll do is make his presence known by standing close and staring at him.

Suave's cell mate has the whole jail on lock. He has a lot of people on the payroll, from inmates to officers. He has almost two years in the building. Rumor has it that he makes anywhere from $10,000 to $15,000 a week from prison. All the heroin that's distributed in there comes from him. He has the whole prison hooked on "BLOCK PARTY". Inmates get their girlfriends to smuggle the dope in during visits. In return, he gives them a small cut. He never even sees the dope. They get the dope in, and the inmates turn it over to his lieutenant. The lieutenant distributes it. He charges $60 a bag. That's six times the street value. He makes more money in here than the average guy makes on the outside.

"That's a good nigga right there," Suave whispers.

"Yeah?" she asks, acting unconcerned.

"Yeah, he rich. He got an asshole full of time though. He ain't never going home."

"Why did that officer call him Mayor?"

She refers to D'andre (Officer Jones) as that officer, as if she doesn't know his name.

"That's what everybody calls him. He's from up the hill from us. Everybody in the town calls him Mayor. When the police raided his house, he had like 3 million cash in there."

"Damn," she whispers. "Who are those Chinese ladies?"

"The old lady ain't Chinese, she's Philippine. That's his mother. He's part black and part Philippine. His father is black. The Asian girl is his wifey."

"Oh," she replies.

"Shit, he told me he had two wifeys living with him together in one house."

"Yeah, right!"

"No bullshit. A couple of people told me that."

"They some fools then. That's why he got Chinese girls, cause he know ain't no black bitch in her right mind going for that shit!"

"Nah, the other one was white."

"Where she at now?" Sincere questions.

"He can't speak with her no more. They all got caught up together. They didn't have nothing on the Asian chick, but they had phone conversations with the white chick discussing business. They tried to give her a lot of time for conspiracy."

"Damn, how did she get away?"

"The Mayor told her to put everything on him. He said at first she didn't want to do it, but after he explained to her that he was never coming home, he finally convinced her. She went all the way with it. She got on the stand and testified how it was him and he made her be involved. She told them he threatened to kill her parents if she didn't do what he ordered. She blew it up real big. It didn't matter though, because there was no way he could have beaten the charges anyway. At first, she kept trying to come see him, but he wouldn't come out to the visit hall. He knew if they found out that she was visiting him, they wouldn't believe her statement. How the hell you gone testify on someone and then go visit him? He had to cut her off for her own safety. Dude crazy!"

"Yes, he is," she agrees.

"I asked him which one he loved the most. He told me he loves both of them equally."

"Hmphh," she snickers.

Officer Jones sneakily steps away from the table.

"That nigga gets on my nerves. If I ever run into him on the streets, I'm gone deal with him," he whispers. "Dick-riding ass nigga."

"Later for him," she whispers, trying to change the subject.

For the remainder of the visit, they cuddled and talked. Officer Jones didn't come anywhere near their table.

CHAPTER 17

Two Weeks Later

Sincere returns from lunch. She walks into her spacious office on the 18th floor. She has a terrific view. Her desk faces the big glass picture window. From the angle where her desk is, she can see the entire city.

She walks in and finds, a bouquet of three dozen roses. The aroma of fresh-cut flowers fills the room. She pulls the card from the vase and reads: Happy Birthday, Baby! D'andre.

Yes, today is Sincere's birthday. Earlier today, the mailman delivered a homemade jailhouse birthday card from Suave.

It took a while for her to get used to receiving cheap little gifts from Suave these past months. She was accustomed to getting cars, furs, and expensive jewelry from him.

As she reaches for Suave's card, which she left on the desk, she realizes it's no longer there. The vase is setting on top of the torn envelope, but no card is inside.

She looks around and finds the card in the wastebasket on top of some papers. She is surprised to see a glob of spit in the seam of the card. She knows exactly what that's about. D'andre must have come in and put the roses on her desk. He saw the card and purposely spit in it, then threw it away.

As she bends over to take a sniff of the roses, the phone rings. She answers while reaching for her chair.

"Hello, you have a collect call from…caller please state your name."

"Suave," the caller says.

Sincere seats herself.

"Do you accept the charges?"

"Yes," she replies.

"Happy birthday, baby!" Suave shouts.

"Thank you."

"I love you, Sincere!"

"I love you more," she shouts back.

Suddenly, Sincere feels something drag across her feet. She quickly slides her chair back and she sees the image of a man. It startles her.

"Aghhhh!" she screams.

D'andre lifts his head up from under the desk and places his hand over her mouth.

"Sincere, what up?" Suave asks.

She can't speak because D'andre has such a tight grip on her mouth. She looks down again, but she can't see his face because it is buried underneath her denim skirt. All she can see is the imprint of the top of his head protruding from between her legs.

"Sincere!" Suave shouts.

She finally manages to snatch his hand away. "Huh?"

"What did you scream for?"

"Uh, nothing. I thought I saw a mouse run across my cabinet."

As she utters the lie from her mouth, D'andre is planting kisses up her inner thigh. A tingling sensation runs through her entire body. She begins to get sexually excited.

"Sincere, what up?" he asks furiously.

"Nothing," she replies. "Why do you say that?" she manages to ask.

"You acting funny as hell. What's up with you?"

She tries to answer, but she can't. D'andre has his tongue jammed deep inside her.

"Sincere, what up?" he asks again.

"Nothing, I'm trying to do two things at one time," she admits. "I have so much work to do."

"Yo, I'll call you at home later," Suave says with a

frustrated tone.

Click! He slams the phone down. Sincere knows Suave is pissed, but right now it really doesn't matter to her. D'andre is taking her to ecstasy. She has totally forgotten where she is.

She reclines in the chair and lays her head all the way back as D'andre vacuums her insides. "Ooh," she moans.

What a birthday present!

CHAPTER 18

Two Months Later/April 2003

It won't be long now. Only six weeks and the nightmare will be over.

Suave and Sincere kiss. "I love you, Sincere!"

"I love you more. It's almost over," she whispers while still holding both of his hands.

"I'll call you tonight," he shouts.

"Alright," she replies. "Bye." She spins around and walks away.

As she walks away, he envisions having crazy sex with her. It's been so long, he thinks to himself. He can't wait to get home to make love to her. He feels like he has deprived her of being a woman. He promises to make her feel like the woman that she is.

Her tiny, terry cloth shorts are fitting perfectly, hugging her curves. They barely cover her cheeks. Each time she takes a step, her shorts inch further up the crack of her ass. By the time she gets to the exit, she has a slight wedgie. Seeing her like this makes Suave jealous, but he has to admit that she does look damn good.

Sincere is one of the last visitors still in the building. As she gets close to the door, she hears, "Psstt." She looks back at Officer Schneider with disgust. He then points to the left. Standing in a doorway to her left is D'andre. He gestures with one finger for her to come over to him.

First, she looks around to make sure no one is looking. Then she peeks back to make sure Suave is gone. The coast is clear. The visiting hall is empty.

After the last visitor leaves, she hesitantly walks over

to him. As she passes Officer Schneider, he licks his lips like a pervert.

D'andre opens the door and steps out. Once he gets in front of the doorway, he begins to look around sneakily. "Go inside," he whispers.

"What?" she asks hastily.

"Just go inside. I have something to tell you."

"No, I'm not going in there," she whispers. She looks over at Schneider; he's staring at her thick, beautiful thighs. She rolls her eyes at him. She hates Schneider. He makes her feel so uncomfortable. His eyes look like the eyes of a rapist. He has no shame. He doesn't care if she knows he's watching. She thinks he's so disrespectful.

What Sincere fails to realize is that D'andre has totally exposed her to all of the other officers. They are all aware of the little creep thing her and D'andre have. She's not the only one though. She doesn't have a clue how these officers sit in the locker room and tell all their bedroom secrets that they have with the inmates' women. She doesn't realize that their relationship is a mere joke to D'andre. The officers use these women only for bragging rights. This adds to their fake-player egos. These no-frills ass officers feel like big shit when they get the chance to creep around with the wife of a "name–brand" dude. Being that her man is "somebody" on the street. The officer feels that this gives him status, which boosts his self-esteem.

"Please, just for one minute," he begs.

She finally gives in. She takes one more look to make sure no one is watching. She then squeezes through the cracked doorway. D'andre follows close behind her.

It's pitch black inside the tiny broom closet.

The clicking sound of the lock breaks the silence. Officer Schneider locks the door from the outside.

"What?" she asks.

D'andre is not answering with words. He replies with

a wet kiss. He pins her against the wall as he nibbles on her earlobes.

"No, stop," she whispers as she pushes him away.

Her hands are resting on his chest. He lifts both of her hands up and kisses her palms one at a time. After kissing her right palm, he drags the tip of his tongue from her index finger to her wrist. He bends down slowly. He continues to drag his tongue down her forearm to her elbow, down to her armpit, where he plants soft kisses. He struggles to lift up her tight, terry cloth shirt. Her sport bra lifts up along with the shirt, exposing her beautiful, oversized melons. Her pink, perky nipples stiffen at the touch of his moist tongue. He alternates, teasing one nipple at a time. He then kisses the middle of her chest, then her belly button. He slides her shorts down.

By now, she's really hot and horny. She has totally forgotten about Schneider, who is standing on the outside with his ear glued to the door, listening. She can't resist him any longer. She grabs the waist of her shorts and panties and wiggles them down to her knees.

D'andre gets on his knees in a submissive position. Before she can even get her shorts past her knees, he dives in face first.

After a few soft kisses and deep tongue lashes, he grabs her by her wide hips and spins her around. Her legs are getting weak. She places both hands against the wall and leans on them while her legs are slightly parted. With her shorts and panties wrapped around her shins, it's hard for her to open them any wider.

She moans as he tastes her from behind. She winds her hips in a slow, circular motion. She picks up the pace and starts bucking like a wild horse. Her body quivers as her love juice drips thick drops onto his upper lip. With his hands holding tightly onto her ankles, he continues to please her.

At the conclusion of the short episode they quickly fix themselves up. D'andre taps on the door. Tap, tap, tap. Click!

The door opens instantly.

"Hurry up," Officer Schneider whispers.

D'andre walks out first and Sincere follows. She can feel his eyes glued to her. Reality sets in. Now she feels totally embarrassed. She walks out the door shamefully.

"Sincere," D'andre shouts, as she nears the exit. She turns around. "Call my cell phone when you get in."

She continues to walk without replying. She feels terrible. How did she get herself in a position like this, she asks herself. How can she do Suave like this? She can't believe she just allowed D'andre to disrespect her like that -getting off a quickie in a broom closet. She can't understand what it is. She has never had an affair on Suave. She doesn't know what it is about D'andre that makes her so weak. It can't be the dick; he's only half the man Suave is in that department. Maybe it's the way he uses his tongue. His tongue makes up for his deprivation.

As she starts up the car, she looks up, just as she does after every visit. After the visits are over, Suave runs upstairs to watch her pull off.

She sees Suave waving from the window. She waves back, wearing a cheesy smile as he blows kisses at her. She backs out of the parking lot. Suave is clueless.

She cries the entire ride home. For the first time, she actually feels like a hoe. She feels so bad that she promises herself this was their last sexual encounter. She prays to God that he gives her the strength to stay away from D'andre.

CHAPTER 19

Four Days Later

It's punch-out time -the end of another hectic day. Officer Jones, Officer Schneider, and six other officers are in the locker room prepping themselves to leave the prison.

Officer Jones buttons up his long-sleeved shirt over his uniform shirt. He never steps foot onto the street with his uniform on.

One of the officers is standing in the center of the room telling one of his famous, corny jokes when Jones's cellular phone rings. Jones huddles over and begins whispering. He talks for approximately ten minutes before the others begin to lose their patience.

"Come on, Jones," shouts one of the officers. "Damn, always making love on the phone!"

Jones cracks a slight grin, while pointing his middle finger in the air. Jones hangs up shortly thereafter.

"Where are we going?" asks another officer. "I know, let's go to Chateaus."

"I'm with that," another officer agrees.

It's Thursday, the night they set aside to hang out for a little while after work. They at least try to hook up two Thursdays out of the month. Usually they go to a go-go Bar, have a few beers, shoot pool, and play around with a few girls.

"What do you think about Chateaus tonight? I figure we can go there and have a few drinks. I'm really not for the go-go scene tonight," the officer admits.

Jones hesitates before replying. "Uh, ya'll can go ahead. I got some other plans tonight. I have a hot date."

"Oh, boy! Another date? You've left us stranded four

Thursdays in a row."

"Come on, man," Jones shouts.

"A date with who?" the officer asks. "Don't tell me you're going with Inmate Calloway's wife?"

"Oh, hell no! I had to cut that crazy bitch off! She thought we were going to be together. Chick got four little crumb snatchers with Calloway. What the hell can I do with her? She stopped coming to visit him and everything. I had to tell her to go visit her husband. Shit, he running around here going crazy. I told her he's stressed out over her. She went eight months without seeing old boy. He was on I Wing beating them niggas damn near to death. It came to a point that I had to beg her to come down here just so I could work in peace. Me and him are pretty tight. He talks to me all the time. He really loves that girl. He always asks my advice about her. Little does he know, I'm the guy that he lost her to. He wouldn't think that in a million years. You know, he supposed to be one of them big willies."

"I heard," an officer agrees.

"When he was driving around the way in Mercedes and Jaguars, he didn't have shit to say to me," says Jones. "He didn't even look my way, like I didn't even exist. Now he got so much to say to me. He cried on my shoulder many a nights. He's shot out over her. I see why though. Old Girl got the snapper! Pussy good, but too much drama to go with it. I had to leave her alone after me and her got into a fight at Sammys on City Island."

"What happened?" the officer asks.

"Man, I'm out there with another chick, and who do I see coming in with three other project ass chicks? Calloway's wife! I tried to duck down real low, but she spotted me. Man, she caused a big ass scene! She tried to fight me and the girl I was with."

"Get the fuck outta here?" The officer can't believe his ears. "How can a married woman fight over another man?"

"Brother, them ghetto ass bitches was ready to tear the restaurant up. I was scared as hell for the little chick I was with. They wanted her ass. She's not about no trouble. She's from Sayreville. She ain't ready for no Newark bitches. She ran and left my ass right there!"

The officers laugh hysterically.

"How did you get out of it?" the officer asks.

"I pulled her out to the parking lot and spit some game at her. After that, I busted her ass in my truck, right in the parking lot."

"Yeah?"

"Yeah, sent her ass back in the restaurant with a wet ass!" he says sarcastically. "Calloway love her, too."

"Hey, he should have thought about that while he was on the streets," says the officer. "Them so-called ballers kill me. When they home, they treat the girl like shit, but as soon as they get locked up, they expect them to do the time with them and be faithful."

"Hey man, them young girls 21, 22 years old, pussy hotter than a firecracker, and these dumb ass niggas think they ain't gone fuck. Nigga think just because he locked up, she's not supposed to get horny no more until he comes home. They gotta be fools. Yeah, those kinds of girls like that fast money, but they also need stability. That's something them big willies can't give them. They're here today, gone tomorrow," says Jones.

"Yep, temporary," the officer answers.

"Yep, and that's where I come in!" Jones says. "Brother, you don't know how much I hate drug dealers."

This is his first time ever admitting this openly, but he really means it from the bottom of his heart. In fact, he treats drug dealer inmates worse than any other inmate. It's almost like he has some type of vendetta against them.

"I hate the way they run around like they own the world, looking down on people like everybody is beneath them. That's

Al-Saadiq Banks

why I shit on them every chance I get," Jones admits.

"No bullshit," an officer agrees.

"So, whatever happened to the other girl?" another officer asks.

"I don't know," Jones admits. "I never seen or heard from her after that night. And that's when I said, that's it! I can't be messing around with her like that. I'll fuck around and lose my job for that project motherfucker."

"So, who are you going out with tonight?"

"I'm not telling that," Jones replies with a devilish grin on his face.

"Sincere," Schneider shouts.

"Who?" the officer questions.

"Eaddie's old lady," Schneider replies.

"Oh, yeah? You got that one, too? You get all the good ones."

"Hey, I can't help it if I'm God's gift to women."

"Whatever," the officer shouts.

"Yeah, he love little Mrs. Eaddie," Schneider claims. "He won't share that one. Won't even let me see the tapes he got of her."

"Come on, Jones. Don't tell me you're in love with her?" the officer clowns.

"Love? What is that?" Jones asks sarcastically. "I don't love. I break hearts."

"You love her," Schneider interrupts. "That's why you keep her away from me. You scared if she get some of this white boy, she won't be calling you no more."

"Please," Jones replies.

"Alright, at least show me the tapes then," Schneider begs.

"Nope."

"See, I told you," says Schneider.

"I showed Baker the tapes."

"Yeah?" Schneider asks. He can't believe it. "I'm your

113

favorite white boy and you won't let me see the tapes, but you let Baker see them?"

"Yeah, you got a big ass mouth," Jones claims. "She already said you are disrespectful as hell."

"Baker, how was she?" Schneider asks.

"Whoa, she's something special," Baker replies, with a look of awe on his face. "Talking about a freak! She be busting Jones's little ass. I told him, she's too much woman for him. She need a big nigga like me to manhandle her ass. You should see that big red ass she got! You won't believe it. She act so innocent when she comes here, but boy she ain't hardly camera shy."

"She knows you taped her?" an officer asks.

"Hell no! Are you crazy?" Jones questions.

"Schneider, believe me when I tell you, baby girl got it going on," says Baker.

"Yeah?" Schneider asks. "No wonder he's in love."

"Love? I told you I don't love her. It's all about a nut for me. She does know how to take care of a man though. Old boy taught her well. I get a home-cooked meal anytime I want one. And she passes off them dollars, too. She holds me down between pay periods. All I have to do is put my stress face on and she pulls out the debit card. As a matter of fact, that's why I'm going there tonight. My pockets are a little low. I figure, I'll go over there, eat some Chicken Parmesan, bust her ass, and I'll step off with about $200 or $300, easy. It's that simple!" Jones brags.

"Yeah?" Baker asks.

"How can she resist? Look at me," Jones replies with arrogance.

"Isn't he on his way home soon?" the officer asks.

"Yeah, he doesn't have much time left," Jones replies. "I might let him get some more of that pussy. It all depends on how he acts these next couple of months."

"I can't stand him," Schneider shouts. "When you go

there tonight, bust a nut on her big ass tits for me. I just want to taste her one time!" he says, while licking his lips. "Is it pink?"

"Hot pink," Jones confirms.

"Damn, please Jones, let me see the tapes. I'll pay for your lunch for a whole month."

"That's nothing," Jones replies. "She already does that. I don't play with her. She has to pay for my services," Jones claims.

"Come on Jones, let me see the tapes," Schneider begs.

"Alright, I'll tell you what," says Jones. "Put me on that little snow bunny with the green eyes; you know, McAllister's wife. Let's pull a double with her, and I'll let you see the tapes."

"That's all I gotta do?" he asks. "That's easy. Consider it done. She'll do anything for me," Schneider claims.

"Are you for real?" Jones asks.

"I'm dead serious," says Schneider. "All I have to do is say the word and it's done."

"OK, here's a little something to make you speed up the process," says Jones, as he digs into his backpack and pulls out a stack of photos.

The men crowd around as he hands a photo to Schneider. They all stand around with their mouths stretched wide open. They can't believe their eyes. There Sincere is, stark naked in a doggy-style position. They damn near drool as they admire her full spread.

If Suave only knew.

CHAPTER 20

Four Days Later

While in the gym watching an intense basketball game, the Mayor was interrupted by two Correction Officers. They escort him to the conference room, where two Federal Agents were waiting for him patiently.

"So Mr. Mayor, here we go again," the agent says sarcastically.

Both agents are white. They appear to be in their late forties. They're as tough as nails. They are the most popular and the most feared agents in the state. Their names are Cohen and Stuart, but inmates who have dealt with them, nicknamed them Beavis and Butthead. These two agents have been harassing the Mayor from day one.

"Listen man, you know what we're here for," says Stuart. "The keyword to this conversation is cooperation. Can you say the word cooperation?" he asks sarcastically.

The Mayor ignores him.

"Listen, we all know you controlled the street but it's obvious there was someone over you. Listen to the keyword, cooperation, there it goes again. You can cooperate and start deducting some of your time or you can, not cooperate and finish the rest of your life in prison. Right now, you can control your destiny. Don't be a fool. Later for the tough, macho shit. Save that for the prison. Right now, it's just us and you."

The Mayor is acting as if they aren't speaking to him. He's staring at the ceiling with a blank look on his face.

"You help us and we'll help you. All you have to do is give us the big man."

"For the tenth time, ya'll already got the big man. Ya'll

got me!" the Mayor says arrogantly.

"Listen, it's obvious that someone was over you. You had to get the shit from somewhere. If the tables were turned, do you actually think he would do the same for you? Do you actually think, he would do life in prison for your black ass?" Cohen asks.

"I'm not concerned with what the next man will do. I only worry about me."

"You know they're about to ship you to Kentucky, right?" Stuart asks. "That's the roughest prison in the country. I'm trying to save you a trip."

"Man, prison is prison. I'll do my time wherever ya'll want me to do it."

"Ok, tough ass!" Stuart shouts.

"Why are you making this harder for yourself?" Cohen asks. "Just cooperate. Tomorrow is your sentencing date. You will be standing before Judge Goldstein. She doesn't bullshit. You were found guilty of possessing several guns with hollow tip bullets. That can easily get you twenty-five more years. Cooperate; keyword, and we'll override that. You won't even have to step foot in the courtroom. It will get dismissed. How does that sound?"

"Sounds like ya'll want me to snitch. I'm no stool pigeon. I'm a man. I piss standing up. If it's going down, let's get it over with," the Mayor says while looking Cohen directly in the eyes.

"We tried. You wanna gamble, let's gamble! Shit is about to get real ugly. Are you sure this is what you want?" Cohen asks.

"I'm positive. If ya'll are finished with me, I'm out. My team has next."

"Ok wise ass, let's play ball!"

CHAPTER 21

The Next Morning

The Mayor stands before Judge Goldstein. The two agents stand in the back of the courtroom watching closely.

As the Mayor walked through the door, they gave him one final chance to cooperate but he ignored them.

Judge Goldstein is a white, Jewish, older woman, who appears to be in her mid fifties. Everyone knows how racist she is. She gives black men the maximum of any sentence.

While the Judge is reading over the paperwork, she suddenly calls for a recess.

As the people are clearing the courtroom, the Judge calls for the Mayor's lawyer. She instructs him to approach the bench.

The lawyer steps slowly but confidently. The courtroom has cleared out, all except the two agents, the Mayor, the bailiff, the lawyer and the judge.

"Yes Maam?" says the lawyer.

"Listen, I was in the process of sentencing your client to an additional 15 years but I had a change of heart. I'm going to give him a break. You owe me one," she says coldly.

"Thank you Maam."

The lawyer walks over to the Mayor. "I got good news. She's going to give you a break. She says she was about to sentence you to an additional 15 years, but she's going to give you a break."

"Oh yeah, why?"

"Me and her are like that," the lawyer brags. "Me and her son used to golf together."

"OK, OK," the Mayor replies. He then turns to his left and there stands Beavis and Butthead right beside him?

"Mr. Mayor, how are you?" Cohen asks. "You talked real bad to us, yesterday. In fact you were so rude that you hurt our feelings. Me and my partner discussed you for hours. 15 years alone for the guns, maybe 60 years for the murders, and let's not talk about the drug charges. We don't wanna see you go out like this. We are not about talking. We're about making it happen. You know, sort of like you? My partner wanted to give up on you, but I said nah, give him a chance. Maybe if we show him how we can help him, then maybe he won't have a problem cooperating. After recess, you'll see how much juice we have. The judge wanted to finish you but we spoke to her. She's going to deduct at least half of the time she was about to give you. That's how cold my juice is!" he shouts.

The Mayor looks at his attorney. The attorney looks away. He feels belittled. He just bragged about how close him and the judge are and her decision had nothing to do with him.

"You don't have to thank us now. Thank us after she sentences you. Do you know how you can show your appreciation?" Cohen asks.

The Mayor doesn't reply. He just stares coldly into Cohen's eyes.

"Just give us our man," says Cohen. "See, we understand that you have to give a little to get a little. That's how it works. Of course, once you get sentenced the judge can't take back her decision but if you don't cooperate afterwards, its' going to get real ugly for you!" he shouts as they walk away leaving the Mayor and the lawyer alone.

"I thought she was giving me a break because of you? You fucking liar!" the Mayor shouts.

"Calm down, calm down. I thought she was doing me a favor," he claims. "So, what are you going to do?"

"Do about what?" the Mayor questions.

"About the situation."

"Situation, ain't no situation," the Mayor says sarcastically. "I got caught doing what I do, now I'm in jail doing my time the way I'm supposed to."

"Hey man listen, you don't want to fuck around with those guys. They are not to be fucked around with. They play dirty."

"So what are you telling me? Are you telling me to snitch?"

"I'm telling you to do what you have to do, to help yourself."

"I don't believe you! I ain't no fucking snitch!"

"You have me in the middle of this," the lawyer whines. "Not only are you hurting yourself, you're hurting me as well. I don't want to be a part of this."

"Hey man, it's too late. You took the paper, you got the job. We're in this together and we ain't telling, ya dig?"

Ten minutes later the judge restarts the case. The Mayor stands tall as the judge speaks to him. Through the corner of his eye, he sees the agents watching him.

"I hereby sentence you to 3 additional years," says the Judge.

She deducted 12 years off of a 15-year sentence. Now that's what you call a juice card.

"Do you have anything to say for yourself?" she asks.

"Yes, Your Honor!" the Mayor shouts clearly.

"Proceed."

"Give me a new pair of Timberlands and I'll do that shit standing up!" he shouts in a disrespectful tone.

The lawyer shakes his head with disgust. The Mayor just disrespected the judge in her courtroom. His arrogance will cost him dearly.

The judge's face shows sign of anger. "Get that

disrespectful moron out of my courtroom!"

As the bailiff escorts him out of the courtroom, he looks over to the agents and winks his eye. While passing the agents, Stuart whispers the words, "Let's play ball."

CHAPTER 22

Five Months Later

It's September of '2003. Suave was supposed to be released a month and a half ago, but they pushed back his date.

After visit one day, Suave and Schneider got into a heated argument. He called Suave a nigga and attempted to spit in his face. Suave couldn't take it anymore. He slammed Schneider to the floor. If it weren't for the Mayor, there's no telling what Suave would've done to him. They have managed to make this one hell of an experience for Suave.

Today is Sunday. Last night was one amazing experience. Sincere's prayers must have been denied, because her and D'andre made love the entire night. She couldn't stand the thought of being away from him. They did it everywhere: the kitchen, the bathroom, even the sun porch. D'andre sure knows how to bring the freak out of her. He has introduced her to a whole different side of herself -a side she never knew existed. He puts her in positions she didn't know her body could be put in. There's nothing she hasn't tried for D'andre.

With Suave, it's totally different. Suave respects her as his queen. Never has he taken her to the next level. If he knew half of the things she has allowed D'andre to do to her, it would drive him crazy. They say one man's fortune is another man's garbage.

She feels free when making love to D'andre. He makes her feel like his personal porn star. He has officially turned her out. That really wasn't hard to do because she didn't have much experience. Suave was her first and her last until she met D'andre. Sincere lost her virginity to Suave when she was in her teens. She never had the chance to experiment. Suave gave her wings, but D'andre has taught her how to fly.

"I'm gone," says D'andre as he peeks into the bathroom, where Sincere is standing at the sink brushing her teeth. Her nude body is a beautiful sight.

She shakes her head up and down to acknowledge that she hears him. She can't talk because she has a mouthful of toothpaste.

She looks him up and down from head to toe. Her mind takes her back to last night. He was marvelous, she thinks to herself. As she looks at him, she asks herself what her friends would say if they knew what she was doing. She has told only one person about her secret relationship, and that's Mocha. She's the only person who would go for it. The rest of her friends would be totally against it. They would look at her differently. They all think she's such an angel, plus they know how much she loves Suave.

When Sincere first told Mocha about D'andre, Mocha didn't believe it. She said, "Not you, Miss Goody Two Shoes." Mocha was so happy though. She hates the ground that Suave walks on. She says Suave doesn't deserve her and she thinks Sincere is the prettiest girl in the world. She always tells Sincere that she's too pretty to be with him and says that with her looks, she could be going out with a rapper or a ball player. Mocha continuously tries to match Sincere up with friends of her significant others.

When Mocha finally saw D'andre, she was upset though. She told Sincere that hearing her talk about D'andre and then seeing him was something entirely different. She told Sincere that she could have found something better to creep around with -someone more worth it. She doesn't deny his attractiveness, but she says he lacks style. Sincere knows exactly why she says that. Mocha only deals with ballers. D'andre is the total opposite. Mocha would never deal with a square, nine to five- type dude unless he was the president of some corporation or something. Even then, she wouldn't want to be seen with him. It would definitely have to be on the low.

Sincere looks at him standing there. He looks so uncool. He has on some all-white Reebok Classic running sneakers. He has them laced up extra tight. He has on a black Sean John sweat suit. The jacket is his exact size, fitting him just right, but his pants are two sizes too small. They're hugging him extra tight. His butt is exploding out of them, causing it to look like he's wearing a pamper. That's the difference between D'andre and Suave. Suave could wear that exact same sweat suit with some all-white Air Force Ones, and he would look like a Sean John model.

The worst of it all is the $5, off-the-stand, no-name shades he has sitting on top of his curly head. He just knows he's the coolest nigga on Earth.

"Ha, ha," she laughs aloud.

"What's so funny?" he asks cluelessly.

"Nothing," she mumbles, holding a mouthful of toothpaste.

"I'm out. I'll hit ya later!"

Seconds later, the phone rings. Sincere runs to the living room to answer it. Instead of leaving, D'andre stands there holding the door halfway open.

"Hello?" she answers. It's Suave. "Yes," she says. "Nothing," she mumbles, as she sits down on the couch.

D'andre slams the door and walks over to the love seat. He sits down and looks directly in her mouth while she's talking. He's making her feel so uncomfortable. He even has the nerve to cough intentionally, trying to let Suave hear him. She can barely answer Suave's questions. She's giving him one-word answers for every question.

Sincere can see the fury in D'andre's eyes. He gets out of the seat and walks toward her, then snatches the phone from her and hangs it up.

"What are you doing?" she asks.

"Shut up! You gone sit here right in my face and

disrespect me like I ain't even here!"

"What are you talking about -disrespect?"

"Yeah, disrespect! You having a good ole conversation with ole boy. I don't disrespect you like that."

Disrespect, she thinks to herself. He's crazy. How can he talk about disrespect when he's in Suave's house?

The phone rings again. She leans over to answer it. He pushes her back into the seat violently. He then reaches for the cord and snatches it out of the wall.

"D'andre stop," she whispers. Now she's getting nervous. He has a devilish smile on his face.

"D'andre, I think you should leave now."

"Leave?" he asks with a sarcastic tone. "I ain't going no motherfucking where!"

She gets up from the chair and storms to the door. She reaches for the doorknob. Slam! He kicks the door right out of her hand.

She looks back at him. She's shocked. She's never seen him act like this. "D'andre, please leave my house," she begs.

"I'm not going nowhere, I told you."

She reaches for the door once again. As she attempts to open it, he backslaps her and slams the door. She stumbles into the wall, holding her eye. She's scared to death. She doesn't know what to do. His temper has gotten the best of him.

Suddenly, D'andre regains control of himself. He now realizes what he has done. His jealousy has taken over. He suddenly realizes he has strong feelings for her and that she's no longer just another creep thing. His little joke has backfired.

He leans over and tries to hug her, but she pushes him away. The blood from her lip leaks onto the thick, white carpet, leaving a stain. He approaches her again. He leans on her with all his weight. He embraces her tightly. She struggles to fight him off, but he's too strong.

He feels terrible. He puts his finger underneath her chin and lifts her head up toward his face. The blood is now pouring from her lip. He tries to kiss her, but she pulls away. He tries again and again until she finally gives in.

He has charmed his way out of this one. D'andre picks her up from the couch and bends her over the arm of the chair, doggy style. He crawls behind her, grabs hold of her waist, and buries his face inside. Her body yearns for him, but her heart wants to push him away. She can't believe she's allowing him to touch her after striking her.

How can I play myself like this, she asks herself. She cries silently. Tears drip down her face, but pleasure drips from her walls.

She bites down on the sofa's cushion just to keep the noise down as D'andre feasts. This is round two of last night's major event.

And the winner is?

CHAPTER 23

Two Months Later/December '2003

It's finally over. Tomorrow is the biggest day of Suave's life. They'll be releasing him in the morning. He thought this day would never come. He can't believe he's actually going to bring this New Year in at home.

He can't wait to get home to sleep in his own bed. He misses Sincere so much.

"Damn, you outta here tomorrow. I'm going to miss you," says Flex.

Flex managed to get shipped to this side, so he could be with Suave. He's been on this side for almost two months now.

"Knock it off," Suave replies. "You'll be right behind me. You only have a few weeks left."

While Flex and Suave are kicking it, the Mayor is off to the side just dazing into space. He has a blank look on his face. Suave recognizes that look. It's the same look he had when they released his former cell mate, the old guy.

In the little time they've been together, Suave has developed a love for the Mayor. Suave never had the privilege of being around the Mayor on the street. The two of them together would have been a hell of a team. Suave always thinks about that, but then again if they had teamed up, Suave wouldn't be going home tomorrow. He would be doing life with the Mayor.

The Mayor takes it well. His spirits are always up. He acts like it doesn't bother him. He constantly tells Suave how he doesn't regret anything he has done in his life. He said the only thing he wishes he could change is the fact that he never got a chance to get even with the Italians who murdered his father.

He promised himself that he would repay them, even if it's the last thing he does. Now the only way he'll get a chance to get even is if they come on the inside.

"Mayor, what up baby? Why are you so quiet over there?" Suave asks.

The Mayor doesn't reply. He just continues to stare at the wall.

"Mayor, wake up!" Suave shouts.

He finally snaps out of it. "Huh?"

"What are you over there thinking about?"

"Oh, nothing. I'm not feeling too good today."

Flex walks off. The Mayor steps closer to Suave.

"Tomorrow you hitting the streets, huh?"

"Yeah, that's what they say."

The Mayor opens his arms wide for a hug. They hug each other. "I'm going to miss you, my nigga," the Mayor claims, while releasing his tight grip. "So, what are your plans?"

"I'm not sure yet. I'm just going to lay back for a couple of weeks and do nothing at first. You know, just to make up for lost time with my lady. Then I'll find something to get into."

"Something like what?"

"I don't know yet. I'm not sure. I think I'm going legal."

"Legal?"

"Yeah legal. I'm tired man. I don't want it no more."

"Don't tell me this punk ass three and a half years broke you," he jokes.

"Nah, not at all. I was tired before I got in here. I been tired. I just couldn't find nothing big to get into."

"Yeah alright."

"Nah, seriously, I'm done. I gotta couple of dollars saved to invest in something. I just don't know what," Suave admits.

"Knock it off, Suave. You a hustler, you always gone be a hustler. You heard what Jay-Z said, 'I'm a hustler, no correctional facility can change that," he sings.

Suave grins slightly.

"I don't know man. I gotta find something to do," says Suave.

The Mayor extends his hand toward Suave. In between his fingertips is a small piece of folded paper. "Here," he says.

"What's that?"

"Here," he repeats. Suave reaches out for it. He opens the paper and sees a phone number. He doesn't know whose number it is, because there is no name to go with it.

"Whose number is this?"

"Just hold onto it. If all else fails, don't hesitate to dial that number."

"Who is it?"

"It's my connect. Just call him and tell him who you are. He'll do the rest."

At this moment, Suave is overwhelmed. He's actually turning over a million dollar connect. "Why me?" he asks.

"Cause, you a real nigga. I like your style. I just ask you one thing."

"What's that," Suave questions.

"If you plug in to him, make sure you hit me off. Don't forget me. Tighten me up every now and then. I ain't never going home. I can't do nothing with it. Ain't no need in letting the connect go to waste. If you don't hook up with him, all he's gone do is find another nigga to hook up with. I made that nigga rich. He knows he owes me the world. He loves me cause he knows I'm a real nigga. When the feds got me, he was shitting bricks. He thought I was gone to bring him in. All I had to do was tell on him and they would have cut my sentence in half. They begged me to tell on my connect. I would rather die than to snitch, ya'ere me? I already told him about you. I told him not to bring nobody else in, but I know eventually he's going to get with somebody else. It's not about loyalty. It's about money. I blew Block Party up. I can't see another nigga getting rich off of my blood, sweat, and tears. Somebody is going to get rich, it might as well be you. Feel me?"

"Yeah, I feel you. Thanks." Suave is flattered that the Mayor thinks enough of him to turn the connect over, but he has made up his mind. He doesn't want anything to do with the streets. Losing Kilo to the game has really had a big effect on Suave.

Kilo was the only person that Suave ever fully trusted. He even trusted Kilo more than El- Amin. He loves Amin with all of his heart and he knows Amin will never do anything to hurt him, but he can never forget what Amin's former occupation was. Although that was years ago, Suave believes that it's always going to be in his heart. It's embedded in him. Suave's motto is "once a stick-up kid, always a stick up-kid." It's only a matter of how much pressure he's put under before he decides to go back to his old ways. Suave is sure Amin will never flip on him, but there are still certain secrets that him and Kilo shared that he would never reveal to El- Amin.

Meanwhile, at Suave and Sincere's house, Sincere is on the phone with D'andre. This is her first time talking to him since the incident when he slapped her. That's when she realized that the whole situation was getting out of hand. It hurts her to think that D'andre slapped her, and all the time her and Suave have been together, he has never put his hands on her like that.

Up until now, she's been ignoring all his calls. Some nights she has stayed at Mocha's house because he has been sitting in front of her house waiting for her to come home. He has even left some violent messages, threatening her if she doesn't reply. She didn't have a clue it would ever lead to this. The only reason she answered the phone tonight is to let him know that Suave is on his way home and he has to stop calling.

"Why the fuck haven't you been answering my calls?"

"D'andre, listen. Stop talking to me like that. The only reason I answered tonight is to tell you Suave is on his way home tomorrow."

"And?" D'andre interrupts.

"And this has to stop. It's over. We both had fun, but we have to move on."

"Fun? Oh, that's what that was, fun? Do I look like a game -a toy that you just play with, then when you get tired you just throw it away?"

"D'andre, in the beginning you were the one who told me you weren't looking for anything more than fun."

"Well, the game changed! Feelings came into the picture." He pauses. "Sincere, I love you."

This catches her by surprise. "Love? You can't love me. I'm in love with someone else."

"So, you mean to tell me, you don't love me?"

"I have developed feelings for you."

"Do you love me?" he asks aggressively.

"I said I have feelings for you."

"So you don't love me?"

"I can't allow myself to love you. I only love one at a time. I love Suave. He's my world. I feel terrible that I cheated on him, but I was lonely. You caught me at a time when I was vulnerable. The situation made me cheat. It wasn't necessarily you. It was the situation. If he were home, I would never have done that to him. I'm sorry to say it, but under normal conditions, I don't think I would've even given you the time of day."

D'andre is getting furious. "What? You think you too good for me? Miss uppity ass bitch!"

"D'andre, please stop with the name calling."

"No. Fuck you, bitch! You think you something cause your nothing ass, drug dealing ass, piece of shit ass boyfriend coming home. You will need me again. Don't call me when they send his dumb ass away for life! You a dumb ass bitch!"

Click! She hangs up on him.

The phone rings instantly. "Hello," she answers.

"Sincere, I'm sorry for talking to you that way, but I truly love you," he whispers. "How can you break it off like this? I want to be with you. He's not right for you. You're a woman, and he's a boy. You shouldn't be left alone like he left you. He's never going to be anything but a criminal. You deserve more. I'm willing to give you the world. Please Sincere, marry me."

Marry him, Sincere thinks to herself. He's losing his mind. She can't believe he just proposed to her. He's left her speechless.

"Sincere, please don't let it all go down the drain. I know you don't want to turn your back on him, but he should have thought about this when he was running around here breaking the law. He wasn't thinking about you then. Please, I'll give you time to break it off with him. How much time do you need?"

"D'andre, what are you asking me?"

"I'm asking you to marry me."

"I can't marry you. I don't love you. I'm in love with Suave."

"Sincere, please," he begs.

Another call beeps in. "Hold on D'andre, someone is on my other line." She clicks over. "Hello?" It's Suave. After accepting the collect call, she clicks back over to D'andre. "Listen, I have to let you go."

"That's him, right?" he asks.

"D'andre, please."

"Sincere, don't do this. Will you call me after you hang up with him?"

"D'andre, I'm tired. I have to get some rest."

"Well, can I call you tomorrow? Will you be home?"

"I beg you D'andre, please don't do that."

He hangs up on her. She clicks back over to Suave.

"Hello?" she answers.

"What's up, beautiful?"

"Hey, Suave."

"You ready for me? We only got about 12 hours left. I hope you kept it tight for me?"

"You know I did," she replies, feeling terribly guilty as she lies through her teeth.

CHAPTER 24

The Next Morning

Today, Sincere met Suave at the gate. She picked him up in her brand new, white BMW truck. Well it's brand new to him; he's never rode in it. She got it two months ago when she traded in the BMW that he bought her. He was so pleased to see his baby doing her thing. It made him feel good to know that she could hold it down without him.

They shopped the day away. Suave had to update his wardrobe. Besides his clothes being a little outdated, he couldn't fit into one single item in his closet because he gained at least 40 pounds.

Sincere finally convinced him to get his hair cut. The first thing she did was take him to the barbershop. After getting the nappy locks cut off, revealing his curly hair, he once again is the most attractive man in the world to her. She let him keep the beard. He just got it trimmed neatly; he refused to cut it.

It broke his heart to see Uncle El- Amin. He's about 50 pounds lighter than he was the last time Suave saw him. He gets dialysis treatment four times a week. Death is visible in his face. He doesn't look good at all.

Suave didn't even go around the projects to see his boys. He doesn't want them to know he's home. He's determined to stay away from them and the street. He kept the number the Mayor gave him, but he really has no plans of ever using it.

Right now, Suave is laying in his own bed, finally –home, sweet home. Sincere is in the shower. He thought this day would never come.

As he flicks through the channels with the remote, Sincere steps into the bedroom. She's looking sexier than ever. She's wearing a hot-pink Victoria's Secret teddy. All her private parts are exposed. The teddy has cut outs in all the right places. He's getting the full view of her firm breasts and her thick bush. That's exactly what it looks like -a thick bush. Suave likes her to keep it hairy like that. She has her hair pinned up in a bun. She looks like a playboy centerfold, the way she's prancing around in those stilettos.

As she gets closer to the bed, a lump forms in his throat. He's actually nervous. He feels like a virgin all over again. He can't wait to satisfy her and finally relieve himself and her of all those years of sexual tension.

Ring, ring! It's the phone. Sincere picks up her pace. She clumsily runs to the nightstand, almost tripping as she tries to answer it before Suave picks it up. It's too late. He beats her to it.

"Hello?" he answers.

Before Suave went away, he never answered the phone. He could be home all alone, and he still wouldn't answer it. This has to be about his third time answering the phone ever. She always complained about him letting it ring off the hook. Tonight his insecurities make him answer it.

"Hello?" he repeats.

Please God, don't let this be D'andre, Sincere says to herself.

"Hello!" he says once again. Click! The caller hangs up. Suave looks at the phone before hanging it up.

Sincere is 100 percent sure that it was D'andre. That was close.

Sincere dims the lights before slowly strutting toward the bed. Suave stiffens just watching her. It seems as though she's taking forever to get there. He's so anxious.

She finally makes it over to him. She climbs on top of the bed and straddles his body. She has him pinned down to the bed. Her knees are on his shoulders. He can't budge.

She starts off by kissing him passionately for minutes.

135

The anxiety is killing him. He tries to palm her behind, but she applies more of her weight so he can't move. She begins to nibble on his ear. Now she's planting kisses all over his chest.

She slides her body to the foot of the bed. They clasp hands as she traces her tongue over his six-pack.

Suddenly, he gets the shock of a lifetime. His mind runs wild as she deep throats him. He can't believe this. In all the years they've been together, never has she sexed him orally. His mind is asking Why now? But his body is enjoying it. What really shocks him is how good she is at it. She's not moving like an amateur.

The funny part is, Sincere is not giving him her all. She could do a much better job if she could concentrate. Her guilt is distracting her from working to her full potential. She feels terrible. She wonders if he can tell she's been tampered with.

She tongue teases him as she grinds away on his knee. Her moisture plasters his leg. The more she pleases him, the fewer questions he asks himself.

A queen pleasing her king, he utters to himself, as she blows his mind.

She climbs aboard and prepares for a long ride.

Thirty seconds later, Suave releases 42 months of pressure.

CHAPTER 25

One Month Later

It's January 10, 2004 –a new year. That means new resolutions for Sincere and Suave. Sincere is determined to be D'andre free. She has managed to stay out of touch with him, although he calls at least twice a day and hangs up. Suave is beginning to get frustrated. Just the other night, he finally brought it to Sincere's attention. He threatened her. He said if he finds out it's a nigga calling, he's going to kill her and the nigga. It just so happens that every time he answers, the caller hangs up. He's on to her.

Sincere thought about changing the number, but she knows that will make her look guiltier. That would be a dead give-away. She just hopes and prays that D'andre doesn't blow her cover.

As for Suave, he has just been laying back, enjoying his freedom. Not once has he even thought about using the number the Mayor gave him. His mind is set. He's determined to stay away from that lifestyle.

Just the other day, he joined a gym. He did that to keep his mind occupied until he decides what he's going to do. He has no plans to fight. He just trains to stay in shape. He even convinced Sincere to start exercising, so now they wake up extra early every morning so they can get a 20-minute run in. After that, they indulge in a quickie, shower, and out the door they go. It's their routine now. They've been doing this every day for almost two weeks. Normally, Suave drops her off at work and comes home until it's time to pick her up from work. After he picks her up, she drives him to the gym, where he spends approximately three hours. He doesn't get in until about 9 o' clock every night.

Right now, they're on their way out the door. After he drops off Sincere, he plans to take a ride back to the prison. He promised himself that after they released him, he would never go anywhere near another prison, but he's making an exception. Today is Flex's release date. Flex begged Suave to come and pick him up. Flex is determined to be a part of Suave's life. He's willing to pay any price. At first Suave hated him, but Flex has managed to force Suave to develop a love for him.

"Lock the door, Boo!" Suave shouts. "I'm going to get the car out of the garage." Suave exits and slams the door behind him.

The wind smacks him in the face as he steps onto the porch. Today is the coldest day so far. He can see his breath as he exhales. Icicles dangle from the porch. Today has to be a record breaker. It's only 7 degrees outside.

As he steps off the porch, he notices an old, raggedy Ford Explorer with dark-tinted windows parked across the street. It catches his attention, because he's never seen it parked on the block before. Suave pays close attention to everything around him.

As Suave backs out of the garage, Sincere is already standing on the curb waiting for him. She opens the door while the truck is still moving. She hops in quickly. Before backing into the street, he hits the remote to close the garage automatically.

Once he finally gets into the street, the Explorer pulls off in front of him. The windows on the Ford Explorer are so dark that it's impossible for Suave to see inside. Suave trails close behind.

"You ever seen that truck around here before?" he asks.
"What truck?"

"That one right here in front of us," he says as he points to the truck, which is beginning to pick up speed.

"No," she replies, while looking out of the passenger's

window. She hasn't looked at the truck one time.

"Let me see who this is. This shit don't look right.
When I came out, it was parked in front of the house just sitting
there." Suave begins to get nervous. His mind starts to play
tricks on him. Maybe the people who killed Kilo have come for
him, he thinks to himself.

Suave steps on the gas a little bit. As he gets closer, the
light at the corner changes from green to yellow to red quickly.
The Explorer speeds right through the light. Suave slams on
the brakes. He sits at the light feeling confused. He doesn't
have a clue who the driver could be but something about that
truck makes him feel uncomfortable.

CHAPTER 26

Two Weeks Later

There has to be a God. Suave didn't believe it would happen, but it did. Good Muslim has managed to get out of prison. He got away with doing less than 14 years on a 60-year sentence. That's unbelievable. Faith has definitely pulled him through. He has lifetime parole, but at least he's back on the street getting a second chance.

Right now, Suave and Flex are dropping Sincere off to work. After that, they're off to pick up Good Muslim. Suave is just about fed up with Flex. He can't seem to shake him. He stays glued to him from the time he drops off Sincere until the evening. He even follows him to the gym. He doesn't work out; he just watches Suave train. During his sparring sessions, Flex plays the role of his corner man.

Not one day passes without Flex begging Suave to call the connect. He's starving, and he's ready to eat. The Mayor told Flex to try to convince Suave to call the connect. Suave still doesn't want any dealings with it. He is about ready to do something for Flex though. He's tired of having to feed and clothe him.

As they're pulling to the gate, Flex screams. "There he go!"

Good Muslim is standing at the gate. When he spots them, he starts advancing toward the truck. He doesn't have a single bag. All he has in his hand is a Qur'an and his prayer rug.

"What's the deal, my beloved brothers?" he says, as he climbs into the backseat.

"What up?" they reply simultaneously.

"Good Muslim, where your shit at?" Flex asks.

"I left it all behind," he replies. "I split it up amongst the brothers. They need it more than me. I'm back in the world, thank God. I can replace all of that. What have ya'll been up to?"

"Nothing much, just trying to stay out here," Suave replies. "What's up with the Mayor?"

"Oh, speaking of the Mayor, I went to see him before I left. He told me to give you this." Good Muslim opens his Qur'an and pulls an envelope from the middle of the book. "Here."

"What's that?" Suave asks, as he extends his hand for the envelope. He pulls the paper out of the envelope, places the paper against the steering wheel, and peeks at it while cruising. An address is printed on the top, and the Mayor's federal and state number are printed on the bottom. Suave quickly reads the letter.

Suave is shocked at what he has just read. The Mayor has offered to sell the connect's phone number for $100,000. The letter states that he'll turn the Block Party connect over for that price. That's $100,000 for the same connect he offered Suave for free. Suave realizes the Mayor must really have love for him. "Whose address is this?"

"I don't know -some kid. The Mayor told me to tell you to stop by the house and give the kid the letter. He said tell the kid it's important; he really needs to talk to him. He said something about, if you're not going to use the number, then he has to give it to someone who will."

Good Muslim doesn't have a clue what he's talking about. If he did, he wouldn't be taking part in it. Flex and Suave know exactly what he's talking about. They never discuss any illegal activity while he's around. They have total respect for him.

Flex sneakily nudges Suave with his elbow and starts shaking his head in frustration. He knows the Mayor is about to pass along the connect. Flex would do anything to get his hands on that number. The Mayor wouldn't dare turn him onto it. He knows Flex isn't worthy of a connect like that. He's so stupid he would end up blowing the entire operation. Before Flex got released, he practically begged the Mayor for the number. He told Flex if he could convince Suave to call the guy, they all would be all right. Flex hasn't been successful. Now the connect has slipped through his hands. He feels like he was so close. He thinks he could have done it, if he just had a little more time.

"When does he want me to go by there?" Suave asks.

"Right now. He made me promise that we would go as soon as you came to get me," Good Muslim admits.

Flex sucks his teeth in frustration. He's pissed off.

For the entire ride, they all remain silent, each one in deep thought. Good Muslim is so happy to be home. He knows it's a blessing. He's just looking around in amazement. He's been gone for almost 14 years. Nothing is the same as when he left. Every little thing has changed, even the Range Rover that he once drove. The body shapes have changed twice since the model he had.

"I had one of those before I went away," he says as a Rover pulls alongside of them. The old body shape though."

For once, Suave is tempted to ask him what he did to get all that time. Whether a new Rover or an old Rover, Suave knows they cost a lot of money. He has to bite his tongue in order not to ask. Instead, he just sits there and thinks of what could have happened.

Flex is busy thinking of how he can persuade Suave to use the number. This is his only means of making some real money. If Suave doesn't call, he doesn't know what his next step will be. He doesn't have a plan B. He never even made any money on the street. He doesn't know the first thing about hustling. Just hearing the stories that Suave and the Mayor talked about -how they bragged about getting so much money

-excited him. He was so sure he was about to blow.

"Right here!" Flex shouts, as they pull in front of the house. On the porch sits an older man eating a sloppy-looking, cold-cut sandwich. In the driveway of the house sits a yellow H2 Hummer, and a black Denali is parked way in the back.

The old man stares at them as they're sitting there.

"Ay, old timer. Do you know somebody who goes by the name Ice?" Flex asks.

The old guy turns his head, ignoring them as he continues to gum his sandwich.

"Excuse me, old-timer?"

"I don't know nobody," the old guy interrupts hastily.

"But," Flex manages to get out before the old guy interrupts him again.

"Bang Man, didn't I just tell you, I don't know nobody."

By this time, a young teen-age kid has come onto the porch. He appears to be about 13 years old. He's wearing a red quilted jacket, beige khakis and red Chuck Taylor Converses, and he has a red bandanna tied around his head and his thigh. He comes to the edge of the porch and stares coldly at them.

"What's popping, Homie?" he asks.

That's Blood talk. This kid is no more than 13 or 14 years old, and he's already gangbanging.

"Ahmir, what the fuck did I tell you about talking that gang shit around me?" the old-timer asks the teen-ager. "I know Cash is turning over in his grave," he adds.

The teen-age kid looks at the old-timer with disgust and rolls his eyes.

"Yo Shorty, you know Ice?" Flex asks.

"Bang Man, I told you we don't know no Ice!" the old-timer replies. He's getting pissed off.

Good Muslim rolls down the window. "Excuse me sir, we're not here to hurt him. We're coming in peace. Someone sent us here to relay a message to him. We just want to leave this paperwork here with him," Good Muslim explains.

The tension in the old-timer's face eases up. Good Muslim steps out of the truck and works his way toward the porch. They look him up and down. The young kid pays close attention to Muslim's long over-garment, which looks like a dress.

Once he gets there, he extends his hand, which is holding the paper. The old-timer just looks at his hand as it dangles in the air.

"Ahmir, go get Ice," the old-timer whispers.

Seconds later, a short, skinny kid in his early 20s hesitantly walks out the door. A pregnant woman follows him. She appears to be very late in the pregnancy. She's as big as a house.

The kid steps to the bottom step, while another teen-age boy wearing all red helps the woman down the stairs.

"What's up," the young man asks.

"I'm looking for someone named Ice," Good Muslim replies.

The woman stops at the bottom step just to see what's going on. The young man presses an alarm on his key ring. The alarm sounds off. "Desire, go ahead and get in the car," he instructs.

The woman and the young boy walk toward an all-black Mercedes Benz convertible SL 500. As she's getting in, he finally replies.

"That be me. What up?"

"Do you know the Mayor?" Good Muslim questions.

"The Mayor?" he asks with a confused look on his face.

"Yeah, well that's what they call him. He told me to give you this information. He says he needs to get in touch with you. He said it's really important."

Ice looks at the paper. His eyes light up instantly. "Oh, that Mayor! I thought you were talking about the real mayor." he laughs. "Alright bet, good looking out, Money!"

Good Muslim makes his way back over to the truck,

144

while Ice jogs over to his car and peels off recklessly.

Suave paid close attention to Ice as he was running. He noticed a red bandanna dangling from his back pocket. Suave assumes he must be a "Blood" also. Maybe he's the one who turned the kids out?

As Flex watches the car zoom up the block, he realizes it's over for him. He was banking on getting that connect. Flex doesn't know the kid Ice, but judging by the way he's rolling, he looks like he can get it done. He knows the Mayor must be about to pass the connect off to him. Flex is pissed. He was so close to making it happen, but now it's over. That's plan A, B, and C down the drain, he thinks to himself.

Fear sets in. Flex begins to worry about his future. He knows if he doesn't get that connect, things are going to be rough for him. That's his only hope. He was so sure he was about to blow. For a quick second, he hates Suave. He feels like Suave is holding him down from doing what he's trying to do.

At this moment, Flex is thinking only of himself. His primary concern is getting that connect, and he's willing to do that at any cost.

CHAPTER 27

Two and a Half Weeks Later/February 14

The courtroom is packed. People are lined up against every wall.

Today is the last day of the Mayor's murder trial. Win, lose, or draw, he has nothing to gain with this case. Losing this case will only add another 30 years to the countless years he already has.

Suave and Good Muslim are sitting in the back row of the courtroom. Good Muslim suggested they come to show the Mayor some support. Good Muslim also wants to see Tony at work. Good Muslim talked Tony into taking the case, after the Mayor's original attorney gave the retainer fee back and denounced the case. He feared how hard they would make it for him if he couldn't get the Mayor to cooperate.

This is Tony's second big case. The first one was Good Muslim's case. Winning this case will really build Tony's credibility.

The Mayor stands here before Judge Goldstein once again. She promised the Mayor if he ever stood before her again, she would make him pay for the way he disrespected her. Now it's payback time.

The federal agents met with the Mayor two days after that day. To their surprise, he still didn't cooperate. They told him that was his final chance to cooperate, and if he doesn't they will be forced to show him why he should have helped them out.

The Mayor sits nonchalantly as the prosecutor speaks. He stares blankly into the eyes of Judge Goldstein. She has been giving him the dirtiest looks ever since he walked into the courtroom.

Suave glances around the courtroom. His attention is drawn to the first row. An old man, a pregnant woman, and two teen-age boys occupy the bench. The two boys are dressed in all red. Suddenly, Suave recalls where he has seen these faces. These are the people from the house that the Mayor sent them to. This must be the family of the victim.

At the end of the same bench sits a beautiful, petite woman. She's been crying the entire afternoon. Suave instantly assumes that she must be the victim's wife.

The old man pulls her close as he tries to comfort her. The pregnant woman watches them with a look of disgust on her face.

Tony stands up. Everyone's attention is drawn to him. His dress code is so different from that of the typical, stuffy attorney. His expensive jewelry makes him look more like a drug dealer than a lawyer. He gleams as the lights bounce off of his platinum bracelet and diamond-studded watch. He's wearing a short-sleeved, peach-colored linen shirt and dark blue jeans. His shoes take the cake. He's wearing brown alligators trimmed with ostrich. His shoes match his briefcase.

He stands there confidently as he clears his throat. "Your honor, my client would like to say a few words to the victim's family."

The judge acknowledges him with a head nod.

The Mayor stands up slowly. He turns toward the bench, where the victim's family is sitting. He begins to speak. "My condolences go out to Donald Pierce's family. First of all, I would like to say that I am totally innocent in this matter. At the time of Cashmere's death, I was incarcerated. I did not murder him, nor did I have him murdered. I know no one believes me, but please just hear me out.

I have nothing to gain with this case. I'm never going home. I have three life sentences to do. If I lose this case, it will

147

only add another 30 years to my sentence.

I won't deny that we were having an issue prior to his murder. Yes, I could have had him murdered, but I didn't. I respected Cash to the fullest. I could never harm him. His death caught me as a surprise, just like everyone else. He raised me. My older brother and him were closer than brothers.

To his sons, I am not the murderer of your father. Trust me, I know how it feels to grow up fatherless. My father was murdered when I was young. My heart goes out to you.

Whatever the jury decides, I'll take it on the chin like the man that I am, but just know it wasn't me." He turns toward the judge as he slowly seats himself.

All the spectators look confused. The widow begins to weep loud and hard. "You murderer!" she blurts out. "You killed my husband! How could you take my husband from me? You ruined my life."

"Recess!" the judge shouts.

Thirty minutes later, the trial restarts. "I would like to bring out my key witness," the prosecutor shouts.

The courtroom is silent as everyone waits to find out who the witness is.

Suddenly, a man who appears to be in his mid 30s makes his way to the stand. As he swears in, the Mayor watches him with a confused look on his face. Before the man can get seated, the prosecutor starts firing away.

The man states that the Mayor offered him $10,000 to kill Donald Pierce, known locally as Cashmere. He also goes into detail about a few conversations him and the Mayor had prior to the victim's death. He claims that he never got a chance to commit the murder because he got arrested the night before.

The Mayor shakes his head in disbelief the entire time the man is speaking. A few times, Tony had to refrain him from jumping out of his seat.

Finally, it's Tony's turn to cross-examine the witness. He

fires away. Tony is handling himself with so much expertise. He asks the witness a series of questions back to back, barely giving him time to answer. After every three questions, Tony allows him a few seconds to answer. Each time he attempts to answer, he gets tongue-tied.

After ten minutes of pressure, something strange happens. The witness breaks down. He bangs his fist into his forehead. "I can't do this," he says, as he shakes his head from side to side. "I can't!" he shouts.

"What are you talking about?" the judge questions.

"Your Honor, I can't go through with this. I don't know that man, and I don't know the victim."

All the spectators are confused. No one has ever seen anything like this.

"They made me do this!"

"Who?" the judge questions.

He hesitates before replying. "Prosecutors, the prosecutors! They made a deal with me. They told me if I got on the stand and help them put him away, they would help me get off with my own murder case. I never met the man. In fact, I never even saw that man in my life. I'm not even from this town. There was never a conversation or nothing. It was all a set-up."

The people can't believe their ears. The prosecutor stands there in shock. As the man pours his heart out, the prosecutor's face shows signs of anger.

The case is dismissed. The jury agrees that the Mayor is not guilty. Tony has pulled off his second major case. Although this case has no winner, at least the Mayor wasn't convicted unjustly.

The question still remains. Who killed Cashmere? His loved ones will never know.

CHAPTER 28

One Week Later

It's 8:30 in the evening. Suave is just getting home from the gym. Sincere has not made it back yet from work. She had to work late today. Suave's trainer had to bring him home.

After taking his shower, he puts left-overs from last night's dinner in the microwave.

Two minutes later, he sits at the table to eat. He's starving. Working out at the gym really has built up his appetite. Today he sparred seven rounds with some kid who has a big fight coming up. After doing seven rounds with Suave, he did another seven with another guy.

As Suave lifts the chicken to his mouth, the phone starts to ring. He doesn't stop. He continues to bite down. The phone rings eight or nine times, but Suave ignores it. The phone stops, but it starts back up immediately. He ignores it again. After four rings, it stops, only to start right back up.

"Damn!" Suave shouts. He doesn't want to answer it, but it might be important. It could be Sincere. She could have been in an accident or something.

He rushes to the phone, but he just misses it. It stopped ringing after three rings this time. As he's making his way back to the table, it starts to ring again. He rushes back over. He snatches the cordless phone from the base and starts back to the table.

"Hello," he mumbles with a mouthful of food. No one replies. "Hello," he repeats.

"Hello?" the caller replies.

To his surprise, it's not Sincere. It's a male's voice. "Yeah, who is this?" Suave asks.

"Let me speak to Sincere," the caller says boldly.

Suave's heart-beat speeds up rapidly. "Hello?" Suave asks in a confused tone.

"Yeah, let me speak to Sincere."

"Who is this?" Suave asks.

"Is Sincere in?" the caller questions.

"Who is this?" Suave asks.

"Listen man, I'm calling for Sincere!"

"Who the fuck are you?" Suave asks.

"This is Mike. Can I speak to Sincere?"

"Mike who?"

"Mike, just plain Mike. Put Sincere on the phone.

Suave is getting furious. "What is this in reference to?"

"It's in reference to Sincere!"

"Listen playa, I'm going to ask you this one time. How did you get this number?"

"I got it from Sincere."

"From Sincere. Where do you know her from?" Suave asks.

"That's my peoples," he claims.

"Your peoples? Sincere is my girl. Did she tell you about me?"

"Yeah, I know all about you."

Suave can't believe this shit. He wishes he could reach through the phone and beat the shit out of this nigga. It would be worthless though. He's not the problem; Sincere is. If she didn't give him the number, he couldn't have called. Suave knows he can't be mad at him. He has to handle this with Sincere.

"Playa, if you know all about me, then why are you calling my bait (home) disrespecting me?" Suave asks humbly.

"I didn't call there for you," he replies sarcastically. "I called for Sincere."

"Listen money, I don't know who you are or what's going on with you and Sincere, but I appreciate it if you never call here again."

"No, you listen. Sincere gave me the number, and I will continue to call until she tells me to stop!"

"Bro, you're going to take this somewhere else. Right now, me and you don't have a problem, but if you call my house again we will. Whatever ya'll had is over now. I'm home! Don't call no more!"

"Whatever, tell her I called!" Click! He hangs up.

Suave is frustrated out of his mind. He doesn't have a clue who this Mike character is. He can't believe Sincere has crossed him. He wonders how many other niggas she's been dealing with. He suddenly loses his appetite. He throws the plate of food against the wall. The plate shatters into tiny pieces as the hot sauce drips down the wall.

He paces back and forth. Time is creeping by. He can't wait for Sincere to get in. He's so anxious that he decides to call her cell phone.

"Hello?" she answers.

"Yeah, what up baby?" he asks, trying to sound as normal as he can.

"Nothing," she replies.

"Where are you?"

"I'm about ten minutes away," she replies.

"Alright then, I'm here."

He hangs up.

Ten minutes feels more like ten hours. The anxiety is killing him. She's going to be shocked.

Everything is starting to come together now. He now realizes that Mike is the person who has been calling and hanging up on him. Suave doesn't know what he's going to say to her. He just wants to see the look on her cheating ass face.

After about 20 minutes, Suave hears the keys at the door. He hauls ass to the bedroom. He lays across the bed, acting as if he's been watching TV.

Sincere finally walks in. "Hey, Boo!" she shouts.

"Ay," he replies, while still flicking slowly through the channels with the remote.

As Sincere kicks off her shoes, Suave drops the bomb on her. "Mike called," he whispers nonchalantly.

"Who?"

"Mike. He said call him when you get in."

"Who?" she asks again.

"Mike, bitch. You heard me!" His voice startles her. "Don't act stupid, you dumb ass bitch!"

"I don't know a Mike," she claims innocently.

"Well, he knows you."

Suave gets up and walks toward the phone. She sees the fury in his eyes. She backs away from him as he grabs the phone.

"Here, call him back," Suave demands, as he tries to hand her the phone.

She looks him in the eyes and says, "I don't know no Mike."

"Well, call him back and find out why he's lying on you. Shit, that's what I would do. Let a bitch call here asking for me, I'll call that bitch back and find out who the fuck she is. Shit! Here, star 69 the number," he suggests, as he starts to dial. "Here it is: 973-449-5555," he says aloud. "Here, ask for him."

Now Sincere is scared shitless. She recognizes the number. It's not a Mike. It's D'andre. She knows she's in trouble now. Why is D'andre doing this, she asks herself.

"It's ringing. Ask for him."

"No, I don't know a Mike, I told you." She has to stick to her story.

"Here, find out who he is then."

She's looking him in the eyes while silently begging God not to let D'andre answer.

"Fuck it, I'll ask for him!" After ten rings, the answering machine finally comes on. The music in the background is some soft love music. Finally, someone speaks.

153

He's talking in a fake Barry White whisper. Before the answering machine can play all the way out, Suave hangs up and dials again. "He's not answering now. Ya'll probably already talked. He already warned you. You a slick ass bitch!"

"Suave, I don't know a Mike," she says as the answering machine picks up.

"Yo fam, pick up the phone," Suave yells into the mouthpiece. "Why you ain't picking up? That's all right though, she gone tell me who you are, and when she do I'm coming for you. I hope you can back up all that slick shit you was talking. You faggot ass nigga!" He hangs up the phone. "Sincere, who is it?"

"Suave, I don't know a Mike," she whispers.

"Stop your fucking lying!" he shouts as he bangs the phone across her forehead. A speed knot swells instantly over her right brow. "You cheating ass bitch! I should kill you in here. He draws back to hit her again, but she covers her head immediately. She then ducks down and runs out of the room. She runs directly into the bathroom and locks the door. Suave storms out of the house.

D'andre has caused a world of trouble.

CHAPTER 29

The Next Day

Sincere still can't believe D'andre has done this. Suave never came back last night after he dashed out. She tried calling him, but he wouldn't answer. She couldn't sleep a wink. She tossed and turned all night. She even called El- Amin. He said he hadn't seen or talked to Suave. She's clueless where he stayed last night. She thinks he might have stayed at a girl's house. He left with her truck. All night, she pictured him riding around with some girl in her truck. Her guilt is playing tricks on her.

She had to catch a cab to work this morning. Today, she looks terrible. She has on the exact same outfit she wore yesterday. Her eyes are swollen shut from crying all night. She hasn't even showered. Her co-workers look at her strangely as she drags into the office with the same wrinkled suit she left in late last night.

The moment she gets in, she checks her answering machine, hoping Suave has left her a message, but instead she hears ten back-to-back messages from D'andre.

Just as she plays the last message, the phone rings. "Hello?" she answers. No one replies. "Hello!" she shouts.

"Good morning, Sincere," D'andre greets sarcastically.

"D'andre, why are you doing this to me?"

"Doing this to you? What about *me*? What about *us*?"

"There is no us. I told you before, I don't love you. I love Suave!" she cries.

"You don't love him. You're confused. If you loved him, you never would have made love to me. We love each other. Don't you see how good it feels when we make love to each other? Don't you feel the chemistry?"

"D'andre, that wasn't love that we were making. That was lust. In order to make love, you have to love the person."

"So, you're saying you just fucked me?" he asks harshly.

"D'andre, please stop calling my house. You're going to cause a lot of problems."

"Problems for who? You confused; I ain't confused. I know we love each other, and we're going to be together whether you like it or not."

"D'andre, I'll have to call the police and tell them you're stalking me if you don't stop."

"Stalking you? Go ahead and do that. You won't do that. You're not stupid. If you do that, you'll have to explain to your little boyfriend about what we have."

"D'andre, we don't have anything!"

"No, not right now, cause you let your little boyfriend come home and destroy our future."

"D'andre, we never had a future."

"Oh, yes we did. We'll be back together though, as soon as I get him out of the way."

"D'andre, please stop," she begs.

"Stop? I have just begun!" Click! He hangs up, while Sincere cries like a baby. What has she gotten herself into?

CHAPTER 30

One Week Later

Things have been very tense around the house. Suave hasn't spoken to Sincere since the phone call. She has made many attempts to talk to him, but he looks away from her as if she's not even there.

She wants so badly to change the number, but that will make her look so guilty. Never did she know that this situation would turn out like this. She's sure Suave will never trust her again. She can deal with that, but she now fears Suave is cheating on her to get even. He's very vindictive. He can hold a grudge forever. He doesn't let anyone get away with anything. He'll get even when you least expect it. He still remembers things that people did to him when he was in kindergarten, and he promises they will pay. The crazy part is that he really means it.

She thought he was going to kill her. When he came back home, he didn't say another word about it. That made her worry even more. She would have rather him beat her brains out and get it over with than to sit around and wait for him to get even. She doesn't know when or how he's going to get even, but she's 100 percent sure he will. She wants to come clean with him, but then he'll ask who the guy is. Once she tells him it's D'andre, Officer Jones, she knows all hell will break out. Then it will definitely be over, so now she has to keep sticking to her story about not knowing who the caller was.

Right now, Suave is on his way to pick up Good Muslim. He needs Suave to drop him off at the train station. He didn't tell Suave where he's going. He just told him he has to step off for a little while.

Suave pulls up to the house and hits the horn. When Good Muslim walks out, Suave almost doesn't recognize him. He has traded in his Muslim attire for some hip-hop urban gear and exchanged his kufi cap for a low haircut. His hair is full of thick, shiny waves. Suave rarely saw him without his kufi on. He switched his long over-garment into a fruity-flavored, Polo, three-button shirt and a sky-blue Ralph Lauren jean suit. He gave up the sandals. On his feet, he has on beige suede Timberland construction boots. He even trimmed his beard. It's still thick, but he snipped all the loose hairs away. He has it looking shiny and well groomed. Even trimmed, it still extends about five or six inches from his chin.

As Good Muslim hops in the truck, the smell of his oils fills the air. He always wears the same fragrance -a mixture of a bunch of oils, but he won't tell anyone the exact mix. He acts like it's top secret. He calls it Beloved. All he's carrying is a small duffle bag.

"What's up, Beloved?" he greets.

"Damn, E Boogie, I almost didn't know who you were," Suave jokes. He remembers the time Good Muslim's lawyer called him that.

"Knock it off. Abdur Rahman is my name," he says with a stern face. "Don't ever call me that again."

Suave senses the bitterness in his voice. "I apologize; I was only bugging. I thought you weren't Muslim anymore. I see you've switched up on me," Suave jokes.

"Nah, it's cool. I just never want to be associated with that E Boogie character. That was my past. E Boogie got me a 60-year sentence. Abdur Rahman got me a second chance." He smiles. "Islam is not in the clothes I wear. It's embedded in my heart. I am a Muslim, and I will die as a Muslim."

"So, where are you off to, and why such a big rush?"

"I have to get to Atlanta."

"For what? What's down there?"

Good Muslim pauses for a second. "Nothing, I got

something to handle down there."

"Something like what?" Suave doesn't like the sound of this.

"Like some unfinished business, that's it."

Suave can tell he doesn't want to answer, and that's why he keeps pestering him. He's not trying to be nosy. He just doesn't want Muslim to get into any trouble. He has genuine love for him. "What kind of business?"

"Unfinished business," he replies.

"Come on Muslim, you're talking in riddles! You're going to tell me something or you're not getting out of the truck."

"Alright, if you insist. I left some unfinished business out here. I owe some people something. Now I have to repay them."

"Who is it? What do you owe them?"

Muslim stares straight ahead. "Are you going to drop me off or what? Later for the million questions," he whispers.

Suave realizes this is something personal, so he decides to leave it alone. They drive for approximately 15 minutes before Muslim breaks the ice. "Where's Flex?"

"I don't know. I haven't been seeing him much since the day we picked you up. I don't know what's up with him."

Suave is lying. He knows exactly where Flex is. Flex is hanging around a bunch of young dudes from his old area. He's trying to get them to bring him in. He finally realized that Suave wasn't going to call the connect, so he had to find another route.

Minutes later, they arrive at the train station. "Thanks a million," he shouts as he grabs the door handle.

"Hold up!" Suave says. He then digs in his pocket and pulls out a stack of $20 bills. He counts out 25 of them and passes them to Muslim. "Here."

"What's this?"

"A little change for your pocket."

"No thanks, I'm alright," Muslim replies modestly.

"Nah, go ahead. Just hold onto it."

Muslim looks him in the eyes. "Thanks, Beloved." He then gets out and slams the door behind him. "You a real dude!" he shouts through the open window. "Thanks again," he says as he starts to walk away.

"Yo!" Suave shouts. Muslim turns around. "Be careful. I don't know where you're going or what you're going to do, but just be careful. I got love for you."

Muslim smiles and walks away quickly.

Suave doesn't know where he's going, but he doesn't like the sound of it. Good Muslim has a different look in his eyes. Normally Suave sees humbleness in his eyes. Now he sees revenge, but he doesn't know what for.

CHAPTER 31

Later That Day

 Suave, his manager, and his trainer just walked into a little, raggedy, hole-in-the-wall gym. The Police Athletic League owns it.
 The tight little gym is extremely crowded. The foul smell of mildew mixed with sweat fills the air. It has about eight punching bags scattered around and three boxing rings, with people in all three of them.
 Suave is here today to spar with a kid from Delaware. As they walk to the locker room, Suave glances around at the scenery.
 "That's him over there -in the ring over in the corner," the trainer whispers.
 In that particular ring, two huge boxers are sparring. One is a guy about 6 feet 5 inches tall. He's big and muscular. He's wearing a tight tank top, black and white Everlast shorts, and black and white Adidas boxing sneakers.
 The other one is much shorter, but he's as wide as a Mack truck. He's built like an action figure. He has his shirt off, and he's wearing some tight, black, spandex shorts with white Everlast sneakers.
 You can't see either of their faces because they have padded headgear on.
 "Which one?" Suave asks.
 "The taller one," he replies.
 Damn, this is going to be tough, Suave thinks to himself. They immediately go to the back, and Suave changes into his boxing attire.
 He stands there patiently as his trainer wraps his hands

for him. He's wearing a tight thermal suit. He has on black Pony sneakers with no socks. He copied that style from the great Mike Tyson. Instead of wearing his protective cup under his thermal pants, he has it pulled over top of the thermals.

"Aghh!" someone cries. The noise came from the gym area.

Minutes later, the kid from Delaware comes into the locker room. His manager and his trainer escort him. He's holding his right hand with his left, and his face shows pain. "Aghh," he cries again. "I think this shit broke," he whispers with agony.

He sits on the bench across from Suave. His trainers begin cutting the tape off of his hand as he moans.

After getting the tape off, he elevates his hand in the air, trying to alleviate the pain. His knuckles are severely distorted. His hand is red and swollen.

"Yeah, she broke," his trainer claims.

"Damn, there goes the big fight!" the manager shouts.

The way his hand looks, there is no way he'll be able to fight two weeks from now. That would have been his big break. It would have been his first big-money fight. It was going to be his first ten-rounder and he was going to score about $70,000 for his pocket.

"So we might as well unstrap, huh?" Suave's trainer asks. "He can't work like that."

"Nah, strap up, it's still work out there. He can move around with the kid Dex was just working with."

"Who is he?" Suave's manager asks.

"Nobody, some non-descript. It's good work though, because he's strong as a bull. That'll get your fighter used to getting hit."

"Be careful with him. He's wild and he fights dirty," the fighter admits.

After taping up, Suave and his camp walk out to the gym area. The dude in the ring has his back facing Suave. Suave notices how chiseled and beautifully sculpted he is.

The guy turns toward Suave. After getting a good look at Suave's face, he immediately turns his head and walks over to his corner. He begins whispering with his corner men. They all look over at Suave as he continues to talk to them.

Suave is confused. He wonders what all the whispering is about. He tries to make them think he's not paying attention to them by shadow boxing. He begins to bob, weave, slip, and jab.

"He's much shorter than you," Suave's trainer states. You have to keep him on the outside. Keep your jab on him. Don't let him get on the inside. He's going to be dangerous on the inside. Keep jabbing and moving. Don't back up. Three-punch combinations, no one or two-piece combinations."

Suave nods his head up and down. Now he's fully focused. He shrugs his shoulders to loosen them up. He bends over to touch his toes. Then he puts his hands on his hips and starts to rotate at the waist.

The kid turns back around and stares directly into Suave's eyes.

Suave squints, so he can get a better view of his opponent's face. It's kind of hard for him to see through the headgear, but the guy does look familiar. Suave inches up a little bit while throwing a series of punches in the air. He's trying to get closer so he can see the guy's face. Suave squints his eyes tighter. Now he recognizes him. Suave is shocked. His heart pounds harder. He can't believe his eyes. It's Officer Jones. Suave freezes for a second.

Officer Jones starts clapping his gloves together extra hard, while giving Suave the dirtiest look he could possibly give him.

Suave starts to shift his body from left to right slowly. He's trying to show a sign of confidence, hoping to intimidate Officer Jones.

Suave has mixed emotions. He's sort of nervous, because

he doesn't know what to expect. He never knew Officer Jones was a boxer. He doesn't know how good Officer Jones is. The other part of him can't wait for the bell to ring so he can tear him apart.

"Come here, Suave," the trainer shouts. "What's the matter?"

"Nothing," Suave whispers. "I know that guy. He's a corrections officer. He used to give me hell down the way."

"Okay, now it's your turn to get even. You got four rounds. That's 12 minutes to punish him. Just stay focused and stick to the plan."

Little does the trainer know, Suave has already forgotten the plan. The only thing going on in his mind is the hell Jones and Schneider put him through. He remembers every incident. He replays them in his head one by one. He's all psyched up now. He can't wait until the bell rings. Now Jones will get what he so rightfully deserves. Suave really wants to see if he's as tough as he acted in the prison. Suave thinks he just hides behind that uniform like the rest of the officers do.

The trainer lifts the water bottle and squirts a hefty amount into Suave's mouth. Suave swishes it from side to side and spits it into the garbage can in the corner of the ring. The trainer then immediately inserts a clear mouthpiece inside Suave's mouth. Suave bites down on it and adjusts it with his tongue while the trainer massages his shoulders.

Officer Jones is staring at Suave without even blinking.

The bell rings. "That's work!" Officer Jones's trainer shouts.

Suave slowly walks to the center of the ring; while Jones trots. They meet at the center. They tap gloves. It's on.

Neither of them has thrown a punch yet. Jones is walking in circles flat-footedly as Suave dances around gracefully. Suave is what you call a stylist. He wants Jones to swing first, so he can see what he's working with.

They continue to circle the ring. "You first!" Suave's

trainer shouts, trying to get Suave to initiate the mix-up. "Go to work!"

The word *work* excites him. He throws a quick jab. It lands directly on the pad of Jones's forehead. Jones tried to move, but the punch got there too fast.

"Again!" Suave's trainer shouts. Suave throws another. The second one was even faster than the first one. It lands in the exact same place. "Three or better," he yells. "Go now!"

Suave throws a jab, which lands on Jones's forehead. He follows it with a left cross, which lands on Jones's cheekbone. He finishes the combination with a strong right hook, which lands on the left side of the headgear, in the ear area.

"Stick and move," the trainer shouts. Jones is coming right at him. Suave throws another jab to slow him down, but he walks right through it. Then Suave throws the same combo again, but this time he puts more body into it. After the combo, Suave slides to his right side to get out of Jones's reach, but Jones beats him to the step and corners him. Jones throws a left hook.

"Ughh," Suave grunts as the impact of the punch rips right through his headgear. His right ear is ringing. Suave uses three quick jabs to work his way out of the corner. Finally, he throws a strong hook and fades off.

The hook wobbles Jones. His legs cross up on him. Suave manages to slide behind him. Jones spins around clumsily and swings a wild haymaker. Suave slips it and throws a combination -jab, left uppercut, right uppercut, left cross. He finishes with a right hook. In between the left cross and the hook, Jones manages to swing another haymaker. This one lands on Suave's chin. Suave stumbles backwards. He's completely off balance. He collapses clumsily onto the ropes. Jones rushes in for the attack.

Ding, ding! The bell sounds off. Suave has just been saved. He's extremely dizzy. He underestimated Jones. Not only can Jones take a hit, but he also can dish one out. He might not throw a lot of punches, but each one he throws counts.

"You alright champ?" the trainer asks.

"Yeah, I'm good," Suave lies.

The trainer can tell he's hurt by the way he's frowning. "You want me to stop it?"

"Hell, no! I'm good."

Even though he's hurt, his pride won't allow him to stop.

"Look at me," the trainer instructs. Suave looks up. The trainer looks in his eyes to see if they're responsive. He then squirts water into Suave's mouth.

The bell rings. Suave jumps up. Jones comes straight at him. As soon as they meet, Jones throws a stiff jab to Suave's head, followed by a quick uppercut to the abdominal area. The jab is painful, but it's nothing compared to the uppercut, which shifts Suave's entire rib cage.

He grunts so loud that Jones hears it and laughs in his face. Suave smiles back at him, trying to make him think he hasn't hurt him, but he doesn't realize that by laughing it off, he's just exposed himself. All fighters know that if you laugh after being hit, that means you're really hurt.

Suave is pissed. He's not dancing as much. The uppercut slowed him down. From the looks of it, Jones has him solved. Suave is a little hesitant about throwing a punch, because he's afraid that Jones will counter. The body shot has taken some of Suave's heart away.

Jones throws a jab followed by a right cross. The cross rips right through Suave's defense and crashes into his forehead. The impact knocks him into the ropes. Jones zooms in for the attack.

"Get out of there, champ," Suave's trainer yells. Suave manages to ease to the right side. As he's stepping away, he throws a short, left uppercut. The punch snaps Jones's head back. Suave then follows up with two quick, consecutive right hooks. Jones stumbles forward and crashes face first into the ropes. Instead of finishing him, Suave spares him by easing away.

Jones regains his composure. They make their way back to the center of the ring. Jones is embarrassed. He feels like Suave has degraded him. Jones anxiously swings a wild haymaker at Suave's head. Suave slips to his right and counters with a swift jab to Jones's forehead. The jab stuns Jones. Suave bends his knees slightly and releases a left cross. "Ughh," Jones almost chokes as the cross crashes into his throat.

As Suave quickly rises, he follows up with a strong, right uppercut. The uppercut lands on the bridge of Jones's nose. Jones's entire head lifts up. Suave has damn near jammed Jones's nose bone into his brain. Suave finishes the combination with a short right hook, which lands flush on Jones's chin bone. Timber! Jones embarrassingly falls face first onto the canvas. The whole gym becomes quiet as everyone watches in awe.

"Hold up," Jones's trainer shouts.

Suave feels great. He has finally gotten even. He's sure Jones won't be able to get up after that combo.

Jones eases into a crawling position while shaking his head from side to side. He's trying to clear his vision. He's extremely dizzy. His body is telling him to stop, but his ego and his legs are telling him something totally different.

Surprisingly, he pulls it off. He stands up slowly. Jones courageously makes his way back to the center of the ring. The spectators impatiently wait for the outcome. Suave can see the fury and the hate in Jones's eyes. Blood is leaking from his swollen nose.

As Jones attempts to advance forward, Suave pops a quick jab just to keep Jones at the tip of his reach. Jones slips the jab, bends at his knees, and fires a hard right cross.

"Aghh," Suave screams as he drops to his knees. He then falls backwards while holding his protective cup. He rolls over onto his stomach. Suave's trainer and manager climb into the ring while the spectators crowd around.

Jones deliberately hit Suave with a low blow to the groin, which finishes him off.

As Suave lays there in excruciating pain, Jones jumps out of the ring, grabs his bag, and storms out of the gym.

CHAPTER 32

One Week Later

Suave has just completed another workout session and is on his way home. He still hasn't said a word to Sincere, but she's fine with that. She's just happy to have him home with her. She knows how close she was to losing him. Having him there is just half of the battle though. The other half is to convince him that she has no idea who Mike is.

D'andre hasn't called her since the threatening phone call to the office. She's worried. She knows he's going to do something; she just doesn't know what it is. He's probably laying low somewhere, putting together a plan to further complicate her life.

Today is Suave's first day coming back to the P.A.L. He's been training at his gym, Red Brick. Today, he came to work with a young amateur kid, who is preparing to fight the New Jersey Golden Gloves Tournament next week. Although the kid is young, he still gave Suave great work.

Jones is nowhere to be found. They say he hasn't been in the gym since the battle he and Suave had.

Suave and Dex (the kid from Delaware) are walking out of the gym. It feels good outside, compared to being cooped up in that hot, funky gym.

Today was Dexter's last day here. Tonight, he's leaving to go back home.

"Here, take my number," Dex suggests. Suave pulls out his cell phone and stores the numbers as Dex calls them out. "I'll be back up this way after my cast comes off."

Dexter's hand is in a cast. That day he sparred with Jones, he broke two of his knuckles.

"Bet," Suave shouts.

"Why don't you come through? You're welcome to come and work out down in our gym. I have a big house all to myself, with two big guest rooms. You can have the lady of your choice. The ladies love me down there. They'll do anything to please me. They treat me like a king. You can use my other car, if you need a car to get around in. I have a brand new 745LI BMW, too. I have the best of both worlds. It's sitting down there in the garage collecting dust. I barely drive it.

Damn, Suave thinks to himself. This dude is eating.

Dex hits the alarm to his brand new Cadillac Escalade. It's jet black with 24-inch chrome rims on it. His manager climbs into the driver's seat, and his trainer jumps into the backseat.

"I got two beautiful cars down there, and I can't drive either one of them with this broke ass hand of mine," he laughs. "Come down and help me out. At least think about it."

"All right, I'll think about it," Suave claims. The offer sounds good to Suave, especially because of his situation with him and Sincere. Maybe some time away would help him clear his head. The vacation might do him some good. Then again, maybe not. It might make matters even worse. If he leaves, that'll give Sincere and "Mike" more time to be together. Suave is definitely confused. Half of him wants to leave her, but the other half would rather die than live without her. He loves her dearly. He needs time to make up his mind.

"Call me," Dex shouts, as they ride off.

Suave walks over to Sincere's truck, sticks his hand inside the window, and opens the door from the inside. He left the windows halfway down, with the keys under the floor mat. He couldn't carry the keys with him because his sweatpants don't have pockets. Besides, a security guard sits at a booth in the center of the parking lot and watches over all the cars in the lot.

After dropping his bag into the backseat, Suave jumps in the driver's side and cruises away.

It doesn't take him any time at all to make it home. As he turns onto Lyons Avenue, he notices a patrol car sitting on the corner of his block.

Suave and the policeman lock eyes. If this had been back in the day, Suave would be preparing to take the chase, but today is a new day. He's clean. He's now a law-abiding citizen. He hasn't done anything illegal since the shooting that landed him 42 months in prison.

The cop busts a U-turn and quickly catches up with Suave. He trails closely behind. Seconds later, he turns on the siren. He's pulling Suave over for no apparent reason. Suave immediately pulls the visor down and grabs hold of the paperwork. He isn't worried at all, because he knows everything is legit and he hasn't broken any laws.

The driver gets out and walks up to Suave's side. Suave boldly sticks his head out of the window. Before the cop gets to the window, Suave snaps. "What are you pulling me over for?"

"Paperwork, please," shouts the officer.

"Why are you pulling me over? It can't be the seat belt. I'm wearing that!"

"Sir, give me your paperwork, please."

Suave shoves it to him. "I didn't do shit," he mumbles. "Just fucking with me." For once, Suave is totally innocent. He feels good to be able to talk back to the police because he knows he's 100 percent clean. "Ya'll ain't got nothing else to do?"

By this time, the other cop is walking toward the truck. He's approaching from the same side. This is a younger cop. He appears to be about 23 or 24 years old. "Step out of the car, sir," he says, as he gets closer to the vehicle.

"For what? I know my rights."

"Sir, please step out."

"First, tell me what for."

The cop reaches for his can of mace. "Sir, please don't make me do this. Just get out."

Suave gets out, but he's still mouthing off. "Ya'll must

171

be bored. Fucking with me for no reason. Ya'll don't have nothing better to do?"

The cop escorts Suave to the back of the truck. "Place your hands on the hatch."

"For what? Am I under arrest?"

"Look, you're pissing me off!" the cop shouts. "Just do as I say."

The first cop pulls out his walkie-talkie and calls in Suave's information. While waiting for the response, he stands close to Suave. He lifts up his leg and rests his foot on the bumper of the truck.

"Can you take your foot off of my truck? I don't even do that."

The cop ignores him. The other cop is searching through the truck.

"Do ya'll have a search warrant? Ya'll can't search my truck. I got all my papers."

"Shut up! You are starting to work my nerves. Just stand there and let us do our job. If you're clean, you don't have anything to worry about. You can drive off and forget this ever happened."

"Rich, cuff him," the officer interrupts. "Cuff him."

Suave thinks he's hearing wrong.

"Hurry up and cuff him."

The first cop draws his gun and grabs Suave by the collar. He pushes Suave face first onto the back window of the truck.

"Hold up! What are you doing? I didn't do shit," Suave claims.

The cop hooks his foot to Suave's shin and sweeps his legs open. Suave tries to resist until the officer kicks him in the ankle.

"Ouch," Suave yells. Suave finally slides his legs apart. The officer forcefully cuffs Suave's hands behind his back, then starts to frisk him.

"What did I do?"

The cop ignores him. He snatches Suave by the cuffs with one hand while he uses the other hand to mash Suave's face against the back window.

"Come on, man," Suave begs.

The cop drags Suave by the cuffs to the front of the vehicle.

"What did I do?" Suave asks again.

The officer who is sitting inside the vehicle rises from underneath the passenger's seat. "What are you doing with this?" he asks as he holds a chrome gun in his hand.

"What? That ain't mine," Suave claims.

"I know, it's mine," he says sarcastically.

"I swear to God that ain't mine," he shouts.

"That's what they all say."

"Listen, that ain't mine. I ain't going to jail for that gun. Honestly, sir!"

"Oh, now I'm sir, huh? I don't want to hear shit. Tell it to the judge."

"I can't believe ya'll doing this to me."

Due to all the commotion, Suave hasn't even noticed the five other police cars that have crept up on the scene. Three of them are regular Newark patrol cars; the other two are unmarked. The unmarked cars are part of the robbery squad. All six officers and the four detectives jump out of their cars and dash over to the truck.

"What have we got here?" the sergeant asks.

"Another punk with a gun, Sarge," the cop replies.

"I ain't no punk, and that's not my gun."

The cop yanks Suave by the cuffs. "Shut up. Speak when spoken to."

"Come on man, that hurts. Them cuffs too tight. Can you loosen them up?" he begs. "Ya'll know I didn't have that gun in there. Ya'll planted that on me. Ya'll fucking with my future."

"You should have been thinking about your future when you put that gun in the truck," says the sergeant. "What were you about to do? Were you about to rob someone? Were you about to kill someone?"

"Officer, please."

"Officer? Do I look like an officer? Do you see these stripes? I'm a sergeant. Don't ever call me an officer!"

"I'm sorry, Sergeant. They planted that gun on me. I just left the Police Athletic League. All them cops there, do you think I'm stupid enough to take a gun there? I'm a boxer. I box for a living," he lies.

No one replies. The cop who searched the car grabs Suave and drags him to the patrol car. "Listen officer, what's your name?" Suave looks to his badge and reads the print. "Jones, Officer Jones. Come on, ya'll know I didn't have no gun in there. Please don't jam me up like this. I'm sorry for talking back, but please don't fuck up my future."

The cop isn't responding. He's acting as if Suave hasn't said a word to him. He jams Suave into the car and slams the door.

The other cop places the gun into a big, plastic zip lock. Suave watches his freedom bounce around in the plastic bag. He knows he can't afford another gun charge. It will be his third gun charge. Several years ago, the police found an old revolver in the back of the projects. They knew it wasn't Suave's, but because he wouldn't tell whose it was, they locked him up for it. Luckily, he only got sentenced to probation. The shooting made his second gun charge, and now this one. That's a total of three gun charges. This is going to be impossible to beat in court. The feds will definitely pick up this case. They're going to charge him with "gun strategy." That's what they call it when you get convicted of three gun charges. That could finish Suave off.

As Suave watches Sincere's truck being lifted onto the flatbed, he asks himself, Is this a coincidence, or do all officers

with the last name *Jones* have it in for me?

CHAPTER 33

Later That Day

Suave has just hung up from talking to Sincere. He's in the Essex County Jail. He told her the entire story about how everything happened. He instructed her to call Brick City Bail Bonds so they could snatch him first thing in the morning.

Sincere truly believes Suave's story. She knows he didn't have a gun. He doesn't even own a gun now. El-Amin took every gun Suave had out of the house back when they first arrested Suave for the shooting.

This whole story sounds weird to her. There's no doubt in her mind that D'andre is behind it. In his last conversation, he said that they will be back together once he gets Suave out of the way. He also said he has just begun. Maybe this was what he was planning to do.

After an hour of dreading the fact that she ever dealt with D'andre, the bell rings. Sincere isn't expecting company. She goes into the hallway so she can peek out of that door, because from the angle of her window, she can't see the porch.

The hall is pitch black. As the door slams behind her, she notices that the front door is open, which makes her uneasy. She backs up, but it's already too late.

"Hey, Sincere," whispers a voice. Startled, she recognizes the voice. It's D'andre. She can't see him at first until her eyes adjust to the darkness.

"D'andre, please leave," she begs.

"Shut the fuck up. Back up in the house before I slap the shit outta you." He shoves her into the door.

"Please don't come in my house," she begs.

He continues to push her, but she's attempting to put up a fight. Slap! She stops squirming. He grabs her by the back of the neck and pushes her inside. Once they get inside the apartment, he uses all his might to push her onto the carpet. She lands on her face. She lays there helplessly, crying like a newborn baby.

"Please leave," she sobs.

He kicks her in the thigh. "I'm not going nowhere. You leave! Didn't I tell you he was going back to jail? He ain't nothing but a criminal."

Now she's sure he's behind it. How does he already know Suave is locked up? She lifts her head up slowly and looks him in the eyes. "How did you know he was arrested?"

"How I know? I, I," he stutters. "My baby brother was the cop who locked him up."

"How could you do that, D'andre?"

"Do what?"

"You framed him."

"No, I didn't. He had the gun in your truck. You see, he don't care nothing about you. He riding around in your truck with a gun on him. Now your truck is under investigation. You know they might keep it, right? It's a chance you might get locked up," he lies. "Especially if he tells them it's your truck and your gun. Do you know how many girls I see in the prisons for messing with these stupid ass drug dealers? They get locked up and put everything on the girl. Shit, everything is in the girl's name -the apartment, the car, everything. It's in your name, whatever is in there is yours."

He's pouring it on thick, trying to scare her.

"You better hope you don't get locked up behind this. That's probably what you need. You ain't gonna be happy until you get your dumb ass locked up chasing behind him. You gone lose your job and everything -fucking with that low-life ass nigga."

"D'andre, I can't believe you would stoop so low."

"Look, you still blaming me. He's the one riding around with a gun in the truck you paid for, and I'm the bad guy. I told

177

you to leave his drug-dealing ass alone. He's a boy. You need a man."

"So I guess you're the man I need, huh?"

"Yeah, but you can't see it right now. One day real soon, you'll see it," he says sarcastically.

"I'm going to tell them you framed him," she threatens.

"Go ahead. They won't believe you."

"Yes, they will. You told me out of your own mouth that you were going to get him sent away. I taped our conversation," she lies.

"Go ahead. If you have that part of the conversation on tape, you must have the rest on tape, too. You know, the part about us not making love and how we were just fucking? You won't dare bring up that tape. If Jamal Eaddie (that's Suave's real name) hears that, ya'll will definitely be finished."

Sincere knows he has a legitimate point. What can she do? D'andre is slowly ruining her life. It's her fault though. She knows she never should have cheated with him in the first place. Now not only has she destroyed her relationship with Suave, but she has also endangered Suave's freedom.

"Please leave my house," she begs.

He races over to her. "I told you I'm not leaving," he shouts as he points in her face. "And don't say it again."

"Please leave," she cries.

He slaps her face twice. She holds her face and takes off, leaving him standing in the center of the living room.

She slams the bedroom door behind her. Baffled, she plops onto the bed. She wants to call the cops, but she knows she'll have to explain to Suave why D'andre was in the house in the first place. She lays there debating. She has the pillow covering her head, so D'andre can't hear her crying. She picks up the phone and dials.

"Hello?"

"Mocha, this me," she whispers.

"What's up? Why do you sound like that?" Mocha

questions.

"He's in here," she whispers.

"What?"

"He's in here," Sincere repeats.

"Who?" Mocha asks.

"D'andre, he's in the livingroom."

"Where is Suave?"

"He's locked up."

"For what?"

"It's a long story. I can't tell you right now. Girl, I don't know what to do," she cries. "He just slapped me. He's acting like a madman. I can't believe this is happening to me. How did I get myself into this situation? What have I done to deserve this?"

"Girl, I'm about to call the cops."

"No, please don't call the cops, please," she begs.

"Girl, that crazy motherfucker might kill you in there."

"Please, Mocha, please."

The door swings open, and D'andre walks in looking like a crazy man. "Who the fuck are you on the phone with?" He runs over to her and snatches the phone out of her hand. He throws it against the wall. She runs to the door, fearing for her life.

"If you call the police, I'll make sure I tell Jamal Eaddie every little detail of our affair. And I do mean everything -oral, anal, everything. I bet you he don't know that his little queen takes it in all holes now, does he? If you don't believe me, just go ahead and try me," he threatens.

He walks up on her real close. She thinks he's coming to attack her again, so she covers her head, but instead he walks right past her. "Remember what I told you," he shouts before walking out of the door.

He slams the door behind him and she immediately locks it. She doesn't have a clue what she should do right now. She just wishes she were dead.

She bangs her head against the door and slowly drops to her knees, crying loud and hard. She knows how she got herself into this situation, but the question is how to get herself out.

CHAPTER 34

Next Day

Sincere was at the county jail bailing out Suave first thing this morning. After they released him, he went straight to his lawyer's office. He has to beat this case; he does not want to go back to prison.

Sincere and Suave have been home all day together, and the only thing that he's said to her was thank you for bailing him out. She's in the bedroom, and he's in the living room flicking through the channels of the television.

The remote slips out of Suave's hand as he dozes off. The noise of the remote banging into the coffee table wakes him out of his nod. He leans over to pick up the remote. It has slid underneath the sofa. He sticks his hand underneath the sofa, but he can't feel it. He then crawls onto the floor and peeks underneath the chair. He sees the remote sitting deep in the back. He sticks his hand to the back and uses his pointer finger to drag the remote to him. The remote has a small piece of paper stuck to it. He picks up the remote along with the paper and gets the shock of a lifetime. In the tips of his fingers, he holds an empty Magnum condom wrapper. He literally loses his mind.

He pops up from the floor and busts through the door into the bedroom. The door crashes into the wall. Sincere jumps out of the bed and runs for cover. She knows he's coming for her, but she doesn't have the slightest idea why. She thinks he's finally going to repay her for the phone call. She's getting so used to getting beat on lately that her normal reaction is to run whenever she senses danger. She squeezes into the corner and crunches up.

"What's this?" he screams as he grips the wrapper with

his fingertips.

She can't tell what it is, because his fingers are hiding the letters. All she can see is *MAG*.

As he approaches her, she can finally view the entire word. She's hoping that her eyes are deceiving her. Where did he get this from, she asks herself. "That's not mine," she says defensively.

"Nah, it's mine," he says sarcastically. "We haven't used rubbers in years, but it's in here."

"I swear!" she shouts. Slap! He knocks her senseless. He then palms her face and rams her head into the wall.

"Suave, I swear," she mumbles, as he continues to bang her head against the wall. She must be getting used to pain, because she has not once moaned. "Suave, I swear," she repeats, as she begins to cry.

"That's it right there. I can't take no more. You cheating ass, unfaithful hoe! I can't believe you!"

The tears are welling up in his eyes.

"Suave, please listen to me."

"Fuck you, bitch!" he interrupts.

Sincere knows she has to say something but she doesn't know where that came from. "Where did you get that from?" she asks.

"Under the sofa, bitch!"

Under the sofa, she thinks to herself. How could that be under there? She just cleaned thoroughly two days ago. She thinks back. D'andre and her have not had sex with each other in about two months. Besides, he couldn't fill out a Magnum in his wildest dreams.

Then it dawns on her. D'andre must have planted the empty wrapper last night. She wants so badly to explain the situation to Suave, but she's really not ready to admit it all to him yet.

Suave starts ram shacking everything.

"What are you doing?" she asks.

"I'm packing. I'm outta here. I ain't dealing with this shit. I can't stand a cheating ass bitch!" The tears are crawling down his face. "How could you do this to me? I never did anything to hurt you. I've been faithful to you. I have given you everything. Is this how you repay me?"

"Please, Suave," she begs as she grabs hold of his hand. He snatches away from her and draws his hand back as if he's about to slap her. At this moment, he wants to beat her to a pulp. He starts to strike her again, but he catches himself. He's furious right now. He knows that if he hits her once, he won't be able to stop. That's against his beliefs; he's totally against hitting women. For years he watched his stepfather abuse his mother – the pregnancy didn't even stop him from beating on her. The last thing he ever wanted to be is a woman beater. The other day was the first time he ever put his hands on a woman. He knows it's wrong, but right now he just wants to get even. He wants to make her feel the pain he feels. How could she betray his trust like this?

He talks himself out of hitting her as he pulls his clothes from the closet.

"Bitch, don't put your filthy hands on me," he mumbles as he grits his teeth. "If you touch me again, I'll kill you. You done had your nasty ass hands all on some nigga's dick! You better not put your hands on me. Who is he? Oh, it's Mike, right? Let me ask you a question. Did you suck his dick, too? You must have, he calling my motherfucking house."

Suave can't take it anymore. His blood is boiling. The thought of her sexing somebody else is driving him bananas. He backslaps her. "You better not gave me no motherfucking AIDS! Oh nah, at least you was strapping up. Here goes the proof right here. I'm still going to get myself checked out tomorrow. I better not have shit. Bitch, you better hope I ain't got shit! If I got anything, I'm going to kill yo slut ass! I swear on my motherfucking life! You trick ass bitch!"

Those words rip through Sincere's soul. She feels

terrible, but what can she say? He won't believe anything that comes out of her mouth right now. She's aware that she deserves whatever he dishes out to her and that she caused this situation. If she could turn back the hands of time, she would have never dealt with D'andre, or anyone else for that matter.

The room is a mess. Suave has destroyed it. He has clothes piled everywhere. He packs a few items into a plastic shopping bag. "I'll get the rest tomorrow. Where is my fucking money at?"

"Suave, please don't leave," she begs.

"Bitch, where my money?"

She's not replying. He begins pulling out her drawers. "Where my fucking money? You better not had spent my shit!" After pulling out all the drawers, he dumps them all one by one onto the floor.

Sincere finally stands up. "Hold up, I'll get it for you."

He continues to dump the drawers while she goes to the closet. She comes back with a strongbox.

From the last drawer falls a stack of envelopes. He stops. He picks up the envelopes and starts to fumble through them. They're letters he sent to her from jail. Two of them are letters to him that she never mailed. The last letter catches his attention because it doesn't have a name on it. He opens it and reads:

Hey, just thinking about you. I can barely work, thinking about last night. Thank you. Thank you for making me feel like a woman. It's been so long. I almost forgot how it feels to make love. I almost forgot how it feels to be touched by a man. You're incredible.

Sincerely yours!

This is the nail in the coffin. She signed it *Sincerely yours,* just like she signed the letters she wrote to Suave. She even dipped the paper in Suave's favorite perfume, not to mention placing the same lip imprint on the bottom.

A teardrop stains the center of the page, as Suave stares at the words *Sincerely yours*. This must be her trademark, he thinks to himself. This is too much for him. As much as he wants to believe this is not true, he can't. He has all the proof he needs. A part of him wants to beat her to death, but he's so heartbroken that he doesn't have the energy.

He turns toward her with his eyes full of tears and just shakes his head at her. "I don't believe you. All the time we got in and this is how you do me?"

Sincere lowers her head with shame.

"Damn, Sincere," he whispers. She tries to reach for him, but he pushes her away. He grabs his shopping bag and the strongbox and proceeds out the door.

"Suave, please," she shouts as he slams the door. He leaves her there crying loud and hard, just like a woman who has lost her only love.

CHAPTER 35

Two weeks later

Suave hasn't been back to the house since the night he found the letter, not even to pick up his clothes. He refuses to go back there. Up until a few days ago, he was staying with El- Amin in the nursing home where he resides. It only took three days before the security guards realized that Suave wasn't leaving at night. They threatened to put El- Amin out if Suave continued to spend the night. For the next two nights, Suave stayed at the Holiday Inn. After that, he had no choice but to call Dex from Delaware. Suave took him up on his offer, and Dex didn't hesitate. Dex and his trainer arrived to pick him up about three hours after they got his call.

Suave needed to get away. He has to get his mind together. He easily could have found an apartment if he chose to. In his strongbox, he has approximately $35,000. He's not hurting for cash; he just wanted to get as far away from Sincere as he possibly could.

He offered to pay Dex rent, but Dex refused. He told Suave he's a guest, and he can't accept money from him. He just wants Suave to put all the pieces of his life back together.

Suave is so confused. He wants to cause someone pain - the same pain she caused him. He can't believe she's done this to him after all the years they've been together. He wonders when it all started. Did it start while he was incarcerated, or had she been cheating all along? He wants to know what kind of character "Mike" is. Is he a 9 to 5- type cat, or is he a baller? Where did they meet? How many times did they fuck? Where did they fuck? Did they do it in the bed where Suave has rested his head? Not in the house that he has risked his freedom just to keep a roof over their heads, he hopes. Is she in love with him? Is Mike a better lover than he is? These are the questions he continuously asks himself day after day. He constantly pictures someone on top of Sincere banging her guts out. The thought of a man abusing her body and purposely causing her pain drives him crazy. His mind is playing tricks on him. At times he clearly hears the loud sound of Sincere's gasps and moans.

Sincere calls him at least 20 times a day. Never does he answer. At times he wants to pick up so he can ask her those questions, but something tells him to avoid her. They say never ask questions that you really don't want the answer to. He also knows that if he picks up the phone and hears her voice, he'll be going back home. He's weak for her. Even though she betrayed him, his heart still wants to go back home. This is the worst situation Suave has ever been in. All the jail time, the beef with the correction officers, the time he spent in the hole, all the ups and downs on the street, the news of his best friend being murdered down south, the news of El- Amin being sick -nothing compares to the feeling he has right now.

Suave needs closure. He won't be satisfied until he sees Mike with his own eyes. He wants to see if this Mike character was really worth risking their relationship for. Suave always warned Sincere about cheating. He told her over and over that men get a kick out of having sex with another man's woman, and once they break up the home, they're done. Once they get the sex, the challenge is dead. Now your home is broken or the bond is ruined, and this guy is somewhere preying on his next victim. God forbid if the woman falls in love with him; she'll find out it was only a game. When Suave drilled her about it, Sincere listened attentively and acted as if she understood him clearly. He wonders where he went wrong.

Suave wonders if he knows Mike. He's sure that it's someone close. Nine times out of ten it is. It's always someone who is right up under your nose -the person you would never suspect, someone the total opposite of what you think your lady would be attracted to. He's almost positive that Mike is some no-frills type dude. El- Amin told Suave that years ago, and he never forgot it. El- Amin said, "You'll be expecting Denzel Washington, and you'll bust her with Gary Coleman." El- Amin always told Suave that love is a dirty game, and he should never get involved with it. Suave didn't listen, and now he has to pay the consequences.

CHAPTER 36

One Month Later/May 2004

This has been a crazy month and a half for Sincere. She has almost lost her mind. She's been taking Tylenol PMs every night just to sleep. She can't even work. She's lovesick. She had to take a leave of absence from her job because she couldn't produce. All she did was sit at her desk and cry for the entire eight hours. The hardest part for her to deal with is the fact that she caused all of this. If it were Suave's fault, she could stomach it better. She would just suck it up like a big girl and move on with her life.

She now realizes even more how much of a good man Suave really is. He has always done his best to provide for her. She never caught him cheating. He doesn't smoke or drink. He doesn't have any babies from past relationships. He's the perfect candidate for any woman. That's what scares her the most. She knows he won't have any problem finding someone to fill her shoes. Sincere knows he truly is a one-woman-man. She knows that if he finds someone, she'll never get the chance to win his love back.

She's definitely going through it. They say you never miss a good thing until it's gone.

Mocha has been staying at the house with Sincere for the past couple of nights. Mocha fears that Sincere will kill herself. Just the other day, Sincere said she doesn't want to live without Suave. Mocha knows those are the words of a suicidal woman.

D'andre sends flowers to the house every other day. He calls about ten times a day. Just yesterday, Sincere got the phone number changed to an unlisted number. Suave never answers the phone when he sees her number, so she was hoping that if he sees a number that he doesn't recognize, he might pick up. It worked the first time, but as soon as he heard her voice, he hung the phone right up. The good thing is, D'andre doesn't have her new number. If that doesn't keep him away from her, then she has no choice but to relocate. She'll move to West Bubble Fuck just to get away from him. As a worst-case scenario, she'll have to call the cops, but she would really hate to do that. Even though he has ruined her life, she still doesn't hate him enough to get him arrested. If all else fails though, she's willing to do whatever she has to do.

CHAPTER 37

One Month Later

Suave is having a tough time getting over Sincere. Dex is so tired of seeing Suave mope around that he decided to take him out just to take his mind off of her for a little while.

Right now, Suave and Dex are on their way back to Dex's house. Suave is driving Dex's luxurious 745 BMW. Suave never would have imagined how smooth this car rides. He has fallen madly in love with the vehicle.

Just pushing the Beamer makes him miss riding in luxury. He hasn't had a new car in over five years. The last new car he bought was a Porsche Carrera. He bought that two years before he went away to prison. Before he checked in, he had a total of three vehicles: the Porsche, a Lexus GS, and a Dodge Intrepid. He used the Intrepid for work. He called that his company car.

A couple of weeks before Suave turned himself in, he sold all his cars to his connect for a total of $85,000. In all actuality, his connect didn't give him cash. He paid him in product. He gave Suave four birds. Even though the birds were worth more than $85,000, it was still fair because of the gamble. The risk evens it out. There was no guarantee that he would make the money back.

Suave gave the four birds to his man Kilo. Suave also gave him $15,000 in cash. Nobody could have told Suave that Kilo wouldn't be around after he came home. He was surely looking forward to coming home to a fortune.

In total, Suave left Sincere with $275,000. She talked him into investing $240,000 of his savings in several savings funds. He can't even touch the money until six years from now.

The CDs have to mature for ten years. Six years from now, those CDs will double in value to $480,000.

At that time, Sincere made Suave believe that investing was the smartest thing for him to do. Suave does recognize how smart it was, but the stupid part was the fact that he put the accounts in her name. Suave has never worked a day in his life, so he couldn't put $240,000 in his own name. They would've investigated him to find out where he got the money.

He invested the money in her name without hesitation. He didn't have a bit of doubt in his mind. He was so sure that she would be his lady for life. Now he feels so foolish. Six years from now, Sincere and Mike will be living it up off of his hard-earned money -money that he risked his life and freedom for. Suave could kick himself up the ass every time he thinks about it. Suave has even had thoughts of killing her just so she can't spend his money. It doesn't sound rational, but right now his life is in a shambles. Luckily, he took the last change he had left before he stepped off that night, or he would have been totally assed out.

Dex is in the passenger's seat, drunk out of his mind. He drank ten shots of 151. He could barely get in the car.

In the backseat of the car are two of the baddest chicks on the planet. Dex managed to talk them into coming home with him. It wasn't that hard to convince them. Like Dex said, the women in this town love him and treat him like a king. He could have left with any woman in the club, but he chose to leave with these two. He told Suave he was not going without them.

They're from Maryland, and they're beautiful. They're about 19 or 20 years old. Dex calls them Night and Day. Day is a short red-bone, about 5 feet 4 inches tall. She has long, auburn-colored hair that falls all the way down to her tiny waistline. She looks like she could be mixed with Indian. She has green eyes and smooth skin. She has a pretty set of thick lips, and her dark lipstick complements her complexion.

She's almost naked. She's wearing a brown, terry cloth halter top and brown, terry cloth coochie shorts. That is definitely the right name for her shorts. Her shorts are so tight you can see her whole coochie print clear as day. She has a tight washboard stomach, and her chest is just right. She definitely has Suave's attention. He wants her badly, but the chances are slim because her attitude is terrible. She's mean and snappy. She really didn't want to leave with them, but the other girl begged her. She's acting so anti-social. Suave tried to ask her name, but she barked on him like, "Listen, I'm not trying to meet anyone. I'm not looking for any friends. I don't need new friends. I have a man, who I am totally happy with. The only reason I'm here is on the strength of my sister." You know how all girls call each other sisters.

He's just been watching her through the rearview mirror. She has a habit of sucking her thumb. Watching her with her tiny finger jammed in her mouth is driving Suave crazy. He finds it so sexy the way she has her lips wrapped around her thumb.

Her beauty disappears once she opens her mouth though. She's a stuck-up bitch. Her "sister," on the other hand, is down for whatever. She's been talking slick the whole ride. She boasts about how she's going to fuck Dexter's brains out. Dex has been challenging her constantly.

By the look of things, Dex is about to do his thing while Suave continues to stress about Sincere.

Suave isn't interested in the other one anyway. She isn't his type. She's tall and slender and as thin as a rail with a flat chest. The only thing she has going for herself is her pretty face. She has brown skin with a long, oval face and a pointy nose. Her eyes are slanted, sort of chinky looking. She has very high cheekbones and a head full of weave that's brown with streaks of blond in it. She's wearing a tiny, micro-mini skirt.

That was a bad decision. The skirt really shows how long and bony she is. She's wearing multi-strapped sandals that tie up all the way up to her knees. She's also wearing a bikini-type top that looks more like a bra. She's as skinny as an Ethiopian. Suave counted every one of her ribs while he stood there listening to her run her mouth at the bar.

As they're riding, Mario Winan's CD blares from the speakers. He's so caught up in the moment that he has replayed the song "I Don't Wanna Know" at least ten times already without even realizing it. The song reminds of him so much of the situation he went through with Sincere cheating on him.

The song fades out, and he immediately restarts it.

"Damn, let the CD play will you?" the girl snaps.

Suave ignores her as he pulls into the driveway of Dexter's house. The girls' eyes almost pop out of their heads as they look at the beautiful, ranch-type house. They begin to whisper.

Dexter is so drunk that he tries to get out of the car while it is still moving.

"Hold up, Dex. You drunk as hell," Suave shouts.

The slim girl laughs hysterically.

Suave gets out first, followed by the slim girl. Dex clumsily climbs out of the car. The other chick hesitantly gets out last. She drags way behind as they all walk to the side entrance.

Dex is taking forever to get the door open.

"Psst!" The snappy chick sucks her teeth. "This motherfucker," she whispers.

Dex finally gets the door open. The girls look around with admiration as they step into the living room. The marble floors catch their attention, and they begin whispering again.

They both glide their hands over the butter-soft, mahogany-colored sectional. Dex grabs the remote and turns on the television. All the attention is drawn to the 60-inch flat screen. Heavy breathing comes through the speakers. Dex has a porno flick in the DVD. How appropriate. The audio is so clear that it sounds like someone is having sex right next to them.

"Let me take ya'll for a tour of the joint," Dex suggests. He then leads them through the house, showing them each room one by one.

Suave is trailing close behind the little mean chick. He wants so badly to say something to her, but he's afraid of how she might react. Suave has the best view. Her round ass is almost bursting through her shorts. She stomps hard as she steps, causing a tidal wave. She's well aware of what she's doing. Suave can tell she's doing it purposely by the way she peeks back at him every few seconds just to make sure he's still looking. She has a tiny waistline with extra-wide hips. Her little round booty is the perfect size. Her shorts leave very little to the imagination.

"And last but not least, this is my basement! This is my favorite part of the house," Dex admits as they all stand at the top of the staircase. "Come on," he urges as he flicks on the light and proceeds down the stairs. They follow close behind.

Halfway down the flight of stairs, Dex flicks another switch and the strobe light begins flashing. The room turns red. The fragrance of burning candles fills the air.

He stops at the last step. The girls glance around the room. It's beautiful. The room is fully laid out. In the center of the floor sits a big Jacuzzi. Directly across the room is another big-screen television. This one is built into the wall. There's a big pool table in one corner, and in the other corner is a bar area with a countertop and four bar stools. To the side of the bar are two booths where you can sit down and have your drinks. He even has a pole extending from the ceiling into the floor. It's the type of pole you normally see in a go-go bar with naked girls sliding down it. The red carpet on the floor has to be at least 12 inches thick.

The tall girl is so amazed that she begins to step into the room.

"No, hold up!" Dex shouts as he snatches her back by

195

her arm. She looks at him with a shocked look on her face. Dexter then points at the floor, where there's a yellow strip separating the wood floor from the carpet. The girl assumes that he doesn't want shoes on his beautiful carpet.

"Oh, my bad," she shouts goofily, as she bends down to take off her shoes. After taking off her sandals, she carefully places them by the bottom step. The other girl bends over and pulls off her shoes also.

The tall chick takes a step onto the rug.

"No," Dex shouts just as her foot sinks into the plush carpet. She's dumbfounded. She has the cheesiest look on her face.

"What?" she asks.

"Read the sign," he replies as he points to a neon sign to the right of them. The sign reads "No clothes beyond the yellow line."

Suave can't believe Dex. Suave hangs out down here on regular basis. He shoots pool by himself all morning, trying to perfect his game. He's seen that sign 100 times, but never has he taken it seriously. He thought it was a joke until now.

"Oh, hell no!" shouts the mean chick. "I wish I would!"

"Hey, that's the house rules. No clothes allowed."

"Oh no, drop me the fuck off. I ain't with this crazy shit. I don't know what kind of perverted shit ya'll on, but get me the fuck up outta here!"

"Calm down," says the slim girl.

"Calm down, my ass! I ain't taking my motherfucking clothes off for these motherfuckers."

"Calm down, Bria," the slim girl whispers.

"No, get me the fuck up outta here."

"Bria, you always doing this shit. Everytime we go somewhere, you always acting like that. We can never go nowhere and chill and have a nice time. You always fucking up my fun."

"Well, stop going out with me," she replies. "Shit, I ain't

196

with this dumb ass shit! One of ya'll gotta take me the fuck home!"

"I'm in for the night," Dex shouts. "I ain't driving to no Maryland, tonight."

Suave isn't saying a word. He really isn't down with the program but he doesn't want to stop Dexter's flow.

"Well, somebody better take me the fuck home!"

Suave feels sorry for her. He really sees that she's not with it. He debates whether or not he should take her home. That would give him more time to talk to her, too. He could kill two birds with one stone.

"If ya'll don't take me home, I'm going to get both of ya'll fucked up!"

With that remark, she just blew her chances of Suave dropping her off.

"Get who fucked up?" Suave asks. These are the first words he has said to her since he asked her name. At first he was going to let her slide with the statement she just made, but his pride won't let him. He hates for someone to threaten him.

"Both of ya'll," she replies.

"Shit, you crazy as hell."

"I bet you I get ya'll fucked up!"

"I bet you won't," Suave challenges.

"Ain't nobody fucking neither one of us up," Dex slurs.

"Okay, don't take me home and see what happens to ya'll."

"Yo Ma, ain't nothing gone happen to me down here," Suave states calmly. "I ain't from around this motherfucker. I don't care about these country ass niggas down here. I ain't never gotta come back down here. These niggas don't want to see me."

"Nobody down here don't care about you either. Come down here with that New York shit if you want to. Yo ass won't make it back home."

"Let me tell you something," Suave says. "I'm the same

197

nigga in town and outta town. I don't change up. If a nigga from my town step out of line, I'll bust his motherfucking head. So what the fuck do you think I'll do to a motherfucker that don't know shit about me? Motherfuckers don't know my name, where I'm from, or nothing."

"Yo, my man down here with me. Ain't shit gone happen to him!"

"Yo ass could get it, too. You ain't nobody. You need to shut your mouth, cause he gone run his punk ass back up north and leave you by yourself. I ain't even gone talk no more. Ya'll better get me the fuck up outta here!"

"See, you fucked up. I was gone take you, but you started popping that goofy shit out your mouth. Now I ain't doing nothing," Suave explains.

"You know what? You don't have to. I swear to God, I'm getting both of ya'll fucked up." She pulls her cell phone out and begins dialing. "My man will come get me. Both of ya'll getting fucked up," she mumbles.

"Hey, do what you gotta do. I'm right here. I'm 250 miles away from home. Where can I go?" Suave asks.

"Chill, Bria," the slim girl whispers.

"Chill my ass! Fuck these corny ass busters."

"Whatever," Suave shouts.

"Especially you, with your punk ass."

"I'll be that, but if you bring a nigga in my face, you better get your black dress ready. Ya'll gone have to bury his ass."

"We gone see," she shouts as she constantly redials the number. Whoever she's calling isn't answering.

"Yeah, we gone see," Suave shouts. "If you love him, you better tell him not to come in my face with that bullshit."

"Chill, Suave. Later for that arguing shit. We down here to cool out and have some fun," says Dex. "So what's up, Slim? You wanna have some fun or what?"

"Yeah, I wanted to, but ya'll bugging."

"It ain't us, baby. It's your peoples. She acting stank as hell."

"Yo Mama stank," Bria yells.

"Bria, please. You going through all this for nothing. Let's just cool out. We can chill here for the night, then leave first thing in the morning. It's already 3 o'clock."

"I ain't staying in this motherfucker!"

"Yo, fuck it. Ya'll gone have to leave. I ain't with this," Dex shouts. "What you gone do Slim? You wit us, or are you leaving with her?"

"I'm staying," she replies hesitantly while looking into Bria's eyes. "We both staying."

"Shit, no I ain't! You staying, I'm outta here," Bria yells while still dialing numbers.

Suave has disrespected the house rules. He's sitting on the sofa fully clothed, flicking the channels with the remote.

Bria sits on the bottom step. She has gotten through to somebody. She's making all kinds of ghetto- hand gestures. It's hard to make out what she's saying because of how loud Suave has the television.

"Come on Slim, that's what I'm talking about," Dex shouts as he starts to undress her. He pulls her bikini top over her head aggressively, almost ripping it off. "Let's get you out of these clothes."

She giggles as he tosses the top across the room. Dex then picks her up in the air and throws her over his shoulder like a sack of potatoes. She laughs as he spanks her butt in a playful manner. He carries her across the carpet. Once he gets her to the bar counter, he lays her on her back and damn near rips off her skirt. The liquor has him acting like a maniac.

Suave peeks from the corner of his eye. Dex is sliding the girl's thong down her legs. She's going with the flow, not putting up a fight. After getting the thong off, Dex lifts it up to his nose and takes a big sniff before tossing it to the floor. Dex then grabs her by the ankles, lifts her legs up in the air, and pins them to her chest. He spreads her legs as wide as he can before burying his face between them. She purrs like a kitten as he tastes her.

The feeling is getting good to her. She grabs the back of his bald head while winding her hips. It must be feeling good to Dex too, because he has sat down on one of the bar stools and made himself comfortable. He's acting like he's at a Thanksgiving feast.

The other girl is still sitting on the step pouting. Suave is pissed. He's sitting there trying to act as nonchalant as he can, while his man is five feet away starring in his own porno movie. Of all the things to be concentrating on, Suave has Sincere on his mind. He wonders where she is. Is Mike in his bed? Are they fucking right now? Does she miss him as much as he misses her, or is she glad that he has left?

"Come here, Playa! Come get some of this," Dex shouts, as he comes up for air. Two seconds later, his face disappears again. She crosses her legs behind his neck to keep him close. There's no way for him to escape as she force-feeds him. She's bucking like a wild horse. It's hard to tell who's making more noise, her moaning or him slurping.

He manages to lift up his head again. "Suave, come on!"

"Nah, I'm good," Suave replies. "Do you."

"Come on, relax your mind, Playa!" Dex backs away from the counter and drags the girl by her hand. Go ahead and take care of my man. Help him relieve some stress," Dex whispers.

As Suave is flicking through the channels, the girl makes her way toward him. Out of the corner of his eye, Suave sees her approaching.

She boldly stands in front of him as he looks her up and down. He can't believe his eyes. He underestimated her. Her slim body is beautiful. She's built like a goddess with the body of a supermodel. Her long, slender legs seem like they never end. Her little doorknocker tits don't even subtract from her beauty.

She glides her hand over her clean-shaven twat. "What's up, Jersey?" she asks as she kneels down to sit on his lap. She sits facing him with her legs straddled over his lap. The feeling of her naked cat pressed against him causes him to get an instant erection. She feels the bulge forming between her legs.

"Whoa, you happy to see me, huh?" she asks as she gropes him slowly. She leans her head closer to his face. He pays close attention to her beautiful brown eyes. She plants soft kisses all over his face. He tries to push her off of him, but she has him pinned to the sofa. She nibbles on his right ear while grinding on him as if she's giving him a lap dance. Part of him is excited and ready to go, but the other part of him is still mad at Bria. He's so pissed at her that he really doesn't want to be bothered. He can't enjoy himself because he doesn't know who she called. He's not scared, but he has to be on point. Dex is the only person he knows around here. If anything goes down and he has to get out of the hole, he doesn't even know how to get around. Dex is his man and all that, but he's from here. If it goes down, who's to say that Dex will stand up for him?

The harder he gets, the harder she grinds. Finally, she rises from his lap. All of a sudden, she falls to her knees and positions herself between his legs. She then reaches for his zipper. He jumps up from the chair and trots away.

"Go ahead," he laughs as he runs away, leaving her on both knees.

"Go ahead, Playa. Let her take care of you," Dex shouts.

"He scared of me," she screams as she chases behind him. He runs around the Jacuzzi, and she follows. She's close behind him. Now he's backpedaling quickly. He's so busy trying to get away from her that he's not watching behind him. He stumbles into the pool table. Now she has him cornered. She pushes him with all her might until he falls backwards onto the pool table. She immediately drops to her knees. He tries to get away, but she is gripping him by his ankles. With her mouth, she nibbles his wood through his jeans. He tries to squirm away, but she has him trapped.

"Go ahead, motherfucker!" Dex shouts. "I know you ain't trigger shy."

She nibbles harder. The teasing is driving him crazy. He finally gives in. She quickly unzips his jeans and reaches inside for her prize. She strokes him for a few seconds before unhooking his belt. She pulls his pants down to his ankles and goes to work. She grabs his hands and places them on the back of her head. Suave is enjoying her mouth. He begins to pump slowly while he simultaneously brings her head closer after every pump. She snatches her head away from him as she stands to her feet. Suave stands straight up in the air.

"That's what I'm talking about, Playa!" Dex shouts from ten feet away. Suave is so caught up in the moment that he has totally forgotten where he is. He has everyone blocked out of his mind except him and her. The sound of 'Sex Me' by R. Kelly echoes throughout the room.

Dex is watching so closely that he's starting to make Suave feel uncomfortable. Suave doesn't doubt his manhood, but he can't concentrate with Dex watching him like that.

The girl pushes Suave onto the pool table. Once he falls back, she bends over, grabs his ankles, and lifts them onto the table. She quickly climbs onto the table.

"Here, catch!" Dex shouts as he tosses a 12-pack of Magnums to them.

She peels a rubber from one of the packets and puts it inside her mouth. She then bends over and puts the condom on him using only her mouth. She jerks her head with a slow motion, back and forth, until the rubber is completely on. She then straddles his body in a riding position. She grabs him with her left hand to guide him inside.

"Aghh," he sighs, as her lips suck him in. She begins to ride. She's moving slowly but confidently, while staring into his eyes. She picks up her pace. Suave starts to flow with her rhythm. He grabs hold of her hips and starts pumping hard. She stops.

"Let me do this. You just sit back and enjoy the ride." She snatches his hands off of her waist and begins to bounce up and down on him like a pro. She's so deep that she's taking all of him without a flinch. The look on her face makes Suave's self-esteem drop. He feels like he doesn't have enough to please her. The worse part is her age. She's too young to be as experienced as she is.

Now she's bouncing even harder. Each time she lands, she purrs like a kitten.

She changes positions. Her ass faces him as she winds her hips slowly.

Dex jumps onto the table. This startles Suave. He keeps his eyes on Dex. He doesn't know what Dex is about to do, but he knows what he better *not* try to do. It's not that kind of party. He begins to second-guess Dex. Maybe he's a homo. Is that why he begged him to come down there, Suave asks himself. Suave glances around the basement, looking for something to beat Dex with just in case he tries something funny. Dex is a big guy. Suave knows he'll have problems beating him with his hands.

The whole situation is making Suave feel uncomfortable. Suddenly, he feels like a freak. He goes limp. He tries to get up from the table, but the girl starts bouncing again. She bounces until he stiffens up again.

Dex stands on the pool table directly in front of the girl. Dex is so tall that he has to bend down just so his head doesn't hit the ceiling.

She reaches for him. She teases him with the tip of her tongue. Dex grabs her by her weave and pulls her closer to him. She gags as he forces himself into her mouth. He's banging her mouth hard and fast. She has to be enjoying it, because the harder he bangs, the harder she bounces down on Suave.

Suave is enjoying it so much that he has forgotten about

203

Dex. He's just watching her ass clap after each landing. She rises up and jumps off the table. She grabs Dexter's hand and pulls him off with her. Suave tries to get up, but she slams him back down. She directs Dex to step behind her. She then bends over for him to take her doggy style. Once he enters, she leans her head over Suave's body. She peels the old condom off of him using her mouth. She then gobbles him up.

Dex is digging deep up in her. He's digging so deep that she has stopped pleasing Suave. She starts to scream loud and hard. In fact, she's screaming so loud that it's hard to tell if she's screaming for more or if she's screaming for mercy. Dex is making a roaring noise. The noise catches Suave's attention. Suave looks over at him. Dex winks and nods his head arrogantly as she screams bloody murder.

Suave watches the girl. He's trying to figure out if it's pain or pleasure. He's so busy watching her that he hasn't even noticed Bria walking toward him. His heart skips a beat as he watches her approach him. She's ass naked. Her pink nipples excite him instantly. Suave is confused.

She stares into Suave's eyes as she stands next to the other girl. She flashes a look of hatred toward him. Suave looks her over from head to toe. Her body is flawless. Even her feet are pretty. Her gold nail polish matches her fingernails, and she's wearing toe rings. Suave has a foot fetish. That's the first thing he looks at on a woman.

He slowly lifts up his eyes until he gets to her thighs. She's closely built. Her thighs are so thick they rub together. You can barely see her bushy cat because her juicy thighs have it covered up.

Suave wonders what made her change her mind. Maybe she got excited watching them, he thinks to himself.

Finally, she speaks. "Ya'll ain't gone be taking tack on my girl like that. Why ya'll gotta jump her?" She then pushes Dex off of the girl. The screaming stops. Bria looks the other girl in the eyes. "Are you alright? Did they hurt you?" she asks in a baby voice.

The girl shakes her head yes with a sad look on her face. Suave gets off of the pool table and stands next to Dex.

"Let me kiss it and make it feel better," Bria whispers as she drops to her knees. Bria spreads the girl's legs apart and plants kisses all over her box.

Suave can't believe his eyes. All that arguing she did just to do this. He didn't have a clue she was this freaky.

The girl grabs a handful of Bria's long, thick hair and drags her onto her feet. She pulls her up with a slow, dominating grip. The girl then makes a head gesture and they both lay on the floor.

After a long, wet, sloppy tongue kiss, they assume the 69 position and begin to please each other. They're putting on one hell of a show. Suave watches closely. He tries to act as nonchalant as he can under these circumstances, unlike Dex, who is busy stroking himself while watching from the sideline.

Bria looks at Suave and gestures for him to join them. He lays down, and they attack him like he's the last man left on the planet. They take turns kissing him from head to toe, just missing his tool. They're avoiding it purposely. They fake him out like they're about to, and then they quickly move away. The anxiety is driving him crazy.

"Yo, Playa!" Dex shouts.

Suave looks up. Dex is standing on top of the pool table ass naked, wood swinging and all. He has his arm extended like he's reaching for Suave.

"Tag me in," he shouts anxiously, like they're a wrestling tag team. "Come on, tag me in!"

Suave humors him by tagging his hand. Dex jumps down, imitating a crazy wrestler. He bends down. He throws a girl onto each of his shoulders and carries both of them to the pool table and dumps them on top of it. He lays them side-by-side. He centers himself between them and spreads their legs as wide as he can. He then dives face first into the slim girl. She strokes his bald head vigorously. While he feasts on her, he pleases Bria with his hand. He forces his big finger deep inside her. After a few seconds, he alternates. The girls kiss each other passionately while he treats them.

Finally, the slim girl pushes him off and jumps off of the table. She drags Bria down with her. They both bend over the table ass up, giving Suave and Dex a formal invitation.

Dex immediately starts pounding the slim girl, while Suave rubs Bria's smooth body. Suave pays her behind special attention as he massages her soft cheeks. She has her name tattooed on her ass. The letters *BRI* are on the left cheek, and the letters *ANNA* are on the right one. Oh, Brianna, he thinks to himself.

Suave peeks to his left and notices that Dex and the girl are not there. He looks behind him, and what does he see? Dex is hanging on the go-go pole. This looks weird to Suave. He's used to seeing pretty, butt naked women slide down those kinds of poles. Never has he seen a big, bald-headed, muscle-bound man on one.

Dex is in the air swinging on the pole while the girl stands there blowing him like a trumpet.

"Look at me, Playa! This is how I get in the club! This is better than the Playboy Mansion! You ain't never partied with a nigga like me!"

Suave can't deny that. Dex has never lied. He really knows how to party. No one could ever have told him Dex was such a freak. He feels bad that he doubted Dexter's manhood, but he didn't know what to think. He's never partied like this, but this is normal for Dex. He told Suave that he sleeps with two women four nights a week. Suave thought he was just talking, but now he's a believer.

Suave has never had this much fun in his life. For once in a long time, Sincere is nowhere on his mind.

Bria lays on the sofa and pulls Suave on top of her. She puts the condom on him and guides him in. She's so tight. He slowly pumps to loosen her up, only giving her half of him. Her breathing is getting heavier and heavier. Suddenly, her lips contract and the suction takes him in. Her beautiful face cringes as he enters her. She now realizes that Suave is too much for her, but it's too late.

He's been waiting for this moment the entire night. He starts to make love to her nice and easy. He's taking his time. He looks down on her beautiful face. He doesn't want to climax too soon. Just looking at her is enough to make him bust off. He closes his eyes to block out the picture. He tries to forget that he's making love to the best-looking girl he has ever had in his life. That works; his urge to bust goes away. She moans as he digs deeper and deeper and deeper. He picks up his pace.

From across the room, he hears the other girl screaming her head off as Dex beats her cooch up.

Suave's ego kicks in. He feels like Dex is pleasing the other girl more than he's pleasing Bria. Suave starts pounding harder. He digs deeper. Her body tenses, but she pulls him closer. Her touch makes him pound even harder.

Finally, he starts to hammer her. "Oh, Suave!" she screams.

The other girl stops screaming due to the loud cry Bria has just made. The noise has even caught Dexter's attention. He stops suddenly.

Suave smiles on the inside as he gives them something to listen to.

He remembers the pain Sincere put him through. He envisions Mike on top of Sincere. His frustration builds up. Later for making love, he thinks to himself. He can't make love to her, because he doesn't love her. The woman he loves broke his heart, turning him into a cold man. He's about to fuck. He's going to make Bria pay for all the pain he's going through right now.

He digs deeper and grinds harder. She places her hands on his chest to regulate how deep he thrusts into her. He snatches her

**hands off of him and starts to jack-hammer her.
"Oh, Suave!" she screams.**

CHAPTER 38

Two Weeks Later

Sincere looks at herself in the full-length mirror, which leans against the wall in her office. She's a mess. Her eyes are swollen shut from crying, and they have dark rings around them from lack of sleep. Tearstains cover her entire face. Her heart is aching badly. She's so lonely without Suave. She wishes she could do it all over again, but this time, she wouldn't fall into D'andre's trap.

She knows Suave will never forgive her, because he's not the forgiving type. Her affair with D'andre has ruined her life. She doesn't know what exactly made her creep with him in the first place. She has never had the urge to cheat on Suave before that incident. Suave is her world. He was there for her when no one else was. If it weren't for Suave, there would be no Sincere. Sincere gives credit to Suave for raising her to be a woman. He taught her everything she knows. He constantly encouraged her to finish school. He helped her build her self-esteem. He made her believe in herself.

Growing up in foster homes deteriorated her sense of self-worth. Suave made her believe that she could be somebody despite what everyone else said. Suave paid her way through college. All the things he's done for her, and this is how she repays him. She can't believe it herself.

Right now, nothing can soothe her pain or fill the empty feeling that has settled in her heart.

She walks over to her desk and looks at the pictures she has posted on her wall. There must be at least 15 pictures of her and Suave together. In the pictures, they look so happy. There are pictures of them together in the Bahamas, in Disney World, in Puerto Rico, and on various cruises that they've taken.

The tears burn her eyeballs as they build up and begin to leak from her eyelids. She reaches over to her desk and picks up a big picture of Suave by himself. It's an old picture of him that he took around the time when they first met. He still looks exactly the same. He's well-preserved. He hasn't aged a bit.

Sincere gets weak just looking at the picture. She starts to cry loud and hard. Without even realizing it, she has picked up the phone and started dialing. Suave hasn't answered her calls in some time now, but she figures it's still worth a try. Just to hear his voice is enough for her.

The phone is ringing. He picks up. Her heart pounds in her chest.

"Hello," says a female voice.

"Hello," Sincere replies with a confused tone.

"Yes?" the girl replies.

"Uh, can I speak with Suave?"

"Excuse me, may I ask who is calling?"

"Tell him it's Sincere."

"Uh, Sincere, as in his ex, Sincere?" the girl asks.

Those words pierce through her heart. *Ex- Sincere*, she thinks to herself. Here she is still madly in love with him. It's only been a short period of time, and he already considers her his ex. "Yes, that Sincere," she shamefully admits.

"Sincere, I would appreciate it if you never call this phone again. Suave and I are happy together. Neither him nor I want to be bothered with you. He told me all about your little affair."

Damn, Sincere thinks to herself. He has told this bitch all of their personal business.

"You had your chance and you blew it. You have already hurt him enough. You left him broken-hearted. I have to repair it and teach him how to love again. Please don't make my job harder than it already is."

"Who are you to tell me not to call?" Sincere asks

hastily.

"You can call me the Love Doctor," she replies.

"Bitch, put Suave on the phone!"

"Sincere, why do I have to be a bitch? I didn't do anything to you. You did it to yourself. It's not my fault that you couldn't be faithful to your man."

"Bitch, put Suave on the fucking phone!"

"Suave doesn't want to talk to you."

"Let him tell me that out of his mouth," Sincere demands.

"Hey, Bay," she whispers. In the background, Sincere hears Suave speaking. He doesn't have the phone to his ear. He's just yelling as loud as he can.

"Bitch, stop calling my phone!"

Click!

This breaks Sincere's heart. She stares at the phone in one hand and then looks at his picture in her other hand. She drops the phone and walks toward the window.

Her mind is blank. Once she gets to the window, she opens the shutter. She pulls the shutter inward and climbs onto the windowsill. She looks at the ground beneath her. She's 12 flights up. From this view, she can see the entire city.

She slowly raises Suave's picture to her lips and kisses him farewell before totally letting herself go. Her body descends rapidly. The wind snatches her breath away. The pit of her stomach drops like she's going downhill on a roller-coaster ride. She tries to scream, but she has no voice. Three stories from the ground, her life flashes before her eyes. She's about to land.

"Ughh!" Sincere screams as she pops up in the bed. Her gown is plastered to her body, and the bed is soaking wet with sweat. She has just had a terrible nightmare.

"Whew!" she sighs.

CHAPTER 39

Three Months Later

Suave just slid back into town early this morning. He hated to come back here, but he had a court date for the gun charge. He has a very tough lawyer, who insists that they are going to beat the case because they didn't have probable cause to search the vehicle.

Suave still hasn't gotten over Sincere and her scandal, but he's managed to put it in the back of his mind. Every now and then he thinks about her, but he quickly erases the thought.

Besides that, things are going well for him. Right now, him and Bria are cruising the town in his brand new, 2004 Porsche truck. It's beautiful. It's grape colored with butter-soft, tan leather interior. He nicknamed the truck Peanut Butter and Jelly. He's the first one to come through this town with one. Everyone stops and stares at them as they breeze through the blocks. His 22-inch chrome rims just add to the beauty.

He paid an arm and a leg for it, but it's okay. He can afford it.

Delaware was a good move for him. No, he's not doing anything illegal. Last month, he signed a contract with Dexter's manager, so he's now officially part of the team.

The manager is filthy rich. He gave Suave a $50,000 signing bonus, and he pays him $800 a week just to train for three hours a day. He even hooked Suave up with his own condo. The cost of living is much cheaper down there. It would cost the same as what Suave pays for a condo down there to live in the "hood" up north. He has two bedrooms. The other bedroom is for El-Amin. Suave is about to move him down

212

there as soon as they change his insurance plan over. The hospital down there doesn't accept Amin's medical insurance. It may take a couple of weeks to get all the proper paperwork in order. After that, Suave won't have any reason to come back to Jersey. What Sincere did may have been a good thing. Suave going to Delaware might have been the best decision he's made in his life. Sometimes you have to give something up to gain something better.

Suave and Bria have been hanging out together almost every day since that wild and crazy night at Dexter's place. Suave has really developed a little liking for her. He knows he shouldn't have gotten attached to her because of how they met, but it's already too late. The question is whether the feelings are mutual?

CHAPTER 40

Weeks Later/Mid-October 2004

The stalking will soon be over. Sincere is about to move into her new apartment.

Her and Mocha have just finished packing the last miscellaneous items away.

A horn is blowing in front of the house. Mocha takes off to the window. She spots the triple-black G-500 Mercedes truck. "That's him! Come look at this truck. This shit is crazy!"

This is Mocha's newest candidate. He's a heavy hitter from Syracuse. He's Spanish. Mocha doesn't discriminate. As long as he has green, American money, he's alright with her.

They just met yesterday, and she already has convinced him to take her for a shopping spree in the Soho section of New York.

They met last night at a birthday party for a New Jersey Nets team player. Mocha is a true groupie. She doesn't miss an event.

"Hurry up, come look at the truck!" she demands.

"Girl, later for that truck," Sincere replies while walking to the window. She peeks out the window and takes a quick glance.

"That shit is hot, right?"

"If you say so."

"If I say so? You don't like it?"

"It's alright. It looks like a mail truck to me."

"A mail truck? Girl, that's a Mercedes truck. That's the hottest thing out here right now."

"Hmphh," Sincere sighs.

Sincere is not impressed with all the glamour. She likes nice things, but she doesn't go to the extreme to get it. She buys expensive things for herself when she can afford it. Mocha has to have it when she wants it. Mocha tries to live her life like a movie star. On her worst day, she looks like she's on her way to a video shoot. Today she looks awesome. She's wearing a black chinchilla vest with the hat to match and black cowboy boots with a black denim shirt and black denim jeans.

She's also wearing her video jewelry, as she calls it. This is a combination of all the jewelry she has accumulated from her niggas. That includes her diamond fluttered charm bracelet with her name spelled out on it, her necklace with a three-karat charm, and the ten-karat friendship ring that she wears on her right hand. Sinister bought her the ring about two months ago as an engagement ring when he proposed to her, but she wears it on her right hand as a friendship ring. Her platinum Cartier is covered with diamonds. He bought her the watch, also.

He loves himself some Mocha. It's hard for Mocha's male friends to compete with Sinister. He *makes* it hard for them. In fact, when she wears this watch on a first date, she usually doesn't get a second one. Depending on who the guy is and what his capacity is, he may get intimidated. Her last victim thought he was doing something big when he showed off his little Rolex with the cloudy little diamonds in it. She broke his heart when she called it a "cute little everyday watch." He almost fainted when she showed him her watch. They've been on several dates since then, but never has he worn that watch again. He's a young kid with a lot of money. He works for some big-time kid across town. Mocha knows she can have the boss, but she's content with the younger kid. Mocha deals with him because she knows she can get anything from him. He'll never tell her no, because his pride won't let him. He doesn't want her to think he doesn't have it. He knows it's a privilege to be with her, so he'll do anything to keep her. He constantly tries to impress her. When he does something for her that he thinks is big and she doesn't respond the way he thought she would, it infuriates him. Soon after, he comes along with something bigger. Mocha knows it won't be long until she drains him of every penny he has, but she couldn't care less.

She has Sinister and the young guy eating out of the palms of her hands. She's sure her Spanish friend will be a little more of a challenge because he has more assets. More assets usually mean more cockiness. Mocha knows she'll have to put in a little more work, but she's sure she can turn him out as well.

"Are you sure you don't want to go? I'll tell him to call up his cousin. He fine as hell. He asked me do I have any friends. He looks way better than my little friend. I wish I woulda met him first. He can't speak a bit of English though. It don't matter. He ain't gotta say a word to me, just put the money in my hand. Shit!"

"Girl, you're crazy. I'm alright," says Sincere.

"Oh, I forgot, you waiting for Suave to come back," Mocha says sarcastically. "You better stop sitting around here waiting for him and move on with your life. You're too pretty for that. As good as you look, you supposed to be chilling with some rich motherfucker, doing you. And you a good girl at that. See, you wife material. I'm always gone be that bitch on the side. I been second all my life, and I don't have a problem with that. As long as they do what I need them to do, when I need them to do it, that's enough for me. I don't want them tired ass niggas. I can get dick from anywhere. You feel me?

"Girl, I done opened all kind of doors for you. I have tried to hook you up with all kind of niggas from big willies to music industry niggas. Remember that football player from the Atlanta Falcons I tried to put you with? He still calls me and asks about you. But no, you was stuck on Suave. Oh, and I ain't even gone bring up Reggie Red. He asks about "Jamie" every time I see him. Now look, Suave ain't nowhere to be found. Then out of all the clowns to creep with, you go and fuck around with that crazy ass geek nigga D'andre. I could kick your ass for fucking with that broke ass buster! I don't know what you were thinking about. You could have been happy as hell right now."

"Mocha, a man don't make me happy. Happiness comes from within."

"Yeah, whatever," Mocha responds sarcastically.

Sincere finally admits to herself that Suave was always right. Mocha is a bad influence. If it were up to Mocha, Sincere would be just as scandalous as she is. She always tried to match Sincere up with a friend of every nigga she met. Mocha is absolutely right; she has introduced Sincere to boxers, football players, hustlers, and music producers, but never has Sincere even considered dating any of them.

Sincere surely realizes what a waste of time it was to creep around with D'andre. Maybe she should have kept in touch with Reggie Red. At least it would have been worth it.

Mocha never respected Sincere and Suave's relationship. Suave hates Mocha more than anyone in the world. He always told Sincere that Mocha has a terrible reputation on the street, and if she continued to hang out with her, people would start to judge her accordingly.

They haven't spoken in about six years. That's how long it's been since he found out that Mocha tried to match Sincere up with a kid from Boston. It wasn't really the fact that she tried to hook her up. Suave is well aware that all women do that. The problem is the dudes she tries to hook Sincere up with. With Mocha being the groupie she is, Suave knows that any guy in her circle has to be somebody important. He always feared losing his woman to some rich cat, but instead he lost her to plain old D'andre. Who would have ever imagined?

The horn beeps again. "Let me go," she shouts. "You can handle the rest, right?"

"Yeah, go ahead. I'm almost done anyway."

"Okay. It's time to make the donuts," she jokes as she

proceeds to the door. "Bye, girl."

"Bye. Don't do nothing that I won't do."

"Girl, I'm going to do everything you won't do, depending on how the bank looks. He's probably a cheapskate. Them be the ones! They got everything -cars, jewelry, house, wife, and they don't want to show a sister no love. He thought he was saying something big when he offered to take me shopping in Soho. I was doing that when I was 15 years old," she laughs. "If he thinks I'll be impressed with a Gucci shoe or a bag, he got another thing coming. This trip will cost him big. When he sees how these Seven jeans are fitting me, he'll have to go to the stash house to pick up some more money," she claims as she glides her hands across her butt.

Her jeans are fitting her perfectly. They're glued to her. The jeans reveal all her beautiful curves.

She turns around and lets Sincere get a view of her juicy, ghetto booty. "Girl, he don't know it's going to cost him at least two grand just to look at this ass, let alone to get some of it," she says sarcastically.

"Girl, get out," Sincere yells.

"Alright, bye bitch!" Mocha shouts as she runs out the house.

She is so anxious that she forgets her shades and she leaves the door wide open.

Sincere struggles to drag the big box to the center of the room. Seconds later, she makes her way over to the door. She pushes it, but a strong force resists it. She pushes it harder, but the door snaps back.

Oh no, she thinks to herself. Please no, she begs.

Yep. It's him. D'andre walks in wearing a devilish smile. He looks around at all the boxes as she backs away from him.

"You leaving me, huh?" he asks.

She acts as if she doesn't hear him.

"I'm talking to you! Some lover you are -moving

without telling me. Where are you moving to? That's fucked up. That ain't how you treat nobody when you in love with them."

"I keep telling you I don't love you."

"Yes, you do. You're just in denial. Where Jamal at? I haven't seen him around."

"Me either."

"Come on, tell me. You know where he's at."

"No I don't, and if I did I wouldn't tell you."

"Don't tell me he left you because of a little argument. I thought ya'll were madly in love. Ya'll should be able to work out any problem. What kind of man is he? Does he run from all his problems?"

"Can you please leave before I call the cops?" she asks calmly.

"Try it," he threatens.

"D'andre, please. You have caused enough damage already."

"I caused? It's me, huh? I did it all by myself, right?" He's starting to raise his voice. "So where the hell is he?"

"D'andre, I don't know."

"He left you, huh? I don't understand how he could just pick up and leave you like that. After all those years you held him down. You didn't miss a visit. See why it don't pay to do no jail time with a nigga? Niggas don't appreciate shit. How he just gone leave you like that? Right now he's probably living with some other bitch while you here stressing over him. That couldn't be me." He's rubbing it in her face. "See, now you have to be with me."

"I'm never going to be with you," Sincere shouts.

"Yes, you will. You love me."

"I will never love you. I don't care if Suave never comes home, I still won't be with you."

"Yes, you will."

"No, I won't!" she shouts.

"Who are you yelling at?"

"I'm yelling at you, D'andre Jones! I ain't scared of you no more. I was only scared that you would ruin everything. You already did that, so I don't have anything else to worry about. There's nothing else you can do to me!"

"Stop yelling at me," he shouts.

She can sense the fury in his voice, but she doesn't care. She's fed up with him. He has ruined everything. "No, get the fuck out of my house!"

Meanwhile, on the other side of town, Suave has just picked up El-Amin. They're on their way back to Delaware.

Right now, Suave is standing outside of the truck, kicking it with some of his old homies from the projects where he used to hang out. They haven't seen him since he's been home. This is his first time coming through here, and he promises himself that this also will be his last time.

They're amazed at his Porsche truck. Suave is bragging to them about his boxing career. While El-Amin is busy ear hustling, Suave's cell phone rings. El-Amin lifts it up and shouts. "Suave, telephone!"

Suave ignores him and continues to run off at the mouth.

"Suave, telephone," he repeats.

"Answer it," Suave replies.

El-Amin presses the button and lifts the phone up to his ear. "Hello?" No one replies. "Hello?" he repeats. El-Amin doesn't hear a voice, but he does hear a lot of commotion. It sounds like someone is tussling over the phone. "Hello?"

He still gets no reply. He suddenly hears the loud sound of someone being slapped. Then he hears a woman screaming. "Please stop," she begs.

Her cry is followed by another loud slap. "Bitch, shut up. I'm not going nowhere," shouts a male voice.

"Please stop hitting me, please. My head hurts. I haven't done anything to hurt you. Why are you putting me through this?" the woman asks. Then comes the sound of two more slaps. "Aghh," the woman cries. "Please stop," she begs.

"Hello," Amin shouts. Who the fuck is this, Amin thinks to himself. He puts his hand over the speaker to muffle it. "Suave, come here."

"Hold up!" Suave replies.

"No, now! Hurry up, you gotta hear this."

Suave sucks his teeth in frustration. He quickly walks over to the truck and sticks his head inside. His face shows signs of aggravation. "What up?"

"Whose number is this?" Amin asks as he shows the display to Suave.

"Oh, that's Sincere. Hang up on that bitch."

"Nah, listen." He lifts up the phone. "They must don't know the phone is off the hook. I been listening to them for the past couple of minutes." Amin presses the speaker button.

"I'm begging you, please leave," she cries. The sound of three loud clapping noises followed by Sincere's cry for help comes through the phone.

"What the fuck?" Suave mumbles. "Somebody whipping her ass."

"You ruined my life. I don't love you! I only love Suave. If I can't be with him, I'd rather die. You might as well take your gun and kill me with it right now! Go ahead and shoot me! I'll never love you!"

There comes the sound of two more slaps followed by a thump. It sounds like he might have banged her across the head with the phone before the dial tone sounds off.

"What the fuck is going on?" Suave asks.

"I don't know. We gotta get over there. Some nigga is beating her ass over you," Amin replies.

That must be Mike, Suave thinks to himself. "We gotta get over there quick!"

"We can't go over there empty-handed. You heard Sincere, the nigga got a gun," Amin explains.

What the fuck is this about, Suave asks himself. "Yo!"

221

Suave calls to the two dudes standing outside the truck. "One of ya'll got a banger with you?"

"Why, what's up?"

"I need it real quick!"

"Yeah, I got one in my car."

"Give it here," Suave shouts.

Both of the dudes run full speed to the car they have parked in the parking lot. They jump in and jump right back out, then they run back to Suave's truck and climb in.

"What up?" they ask as Suave peels out of the lot.

"I don't know yet, but some bullshit going down."

As they're riding, Suave debates whether he should take his boys with him. They'll want answers. They're going to ask what a nigga is doing in his home. He doesn't want to admit to them that Sincere has been cheating on him. He'll be the joke of the town. Everyone knows how long him and Sincere have been together. The "hood" looks at them like the model couple. Until now, they have never been in any drama. Everyone thinks Sincere is the perfect wifey. But right now, Sincere needs him, so he has to throw his pride out of the window.

Five minutes later, Suave turns onto the block. As he approaches the house, the first thing he notices is the raggedy Ford Explorer with the dark-tinted windows. His heart begins to race as he thinks back to the morning when he saw the truck parked in front of the house. Now he realizes that the truck was there for her all the while. He feels like a fool.

He's so anxious that he double-parks in the middle of the street.

"Give me the banger!" he shouts. The kid passes him the gun. As Suave tucks the pistol in his pants, he suddenly gets butterflies in his stomach. He now realizes the trouble this gun can get him into. One more gun charge will finish him for the rest of his life.

He hops out of the truck and heads for the house. All the passengers follow.

The door to the sun-porch is stretched wide open. Suave runs straight through the hall. When he encounters the door to the apartment, he puts his ear close so he can hear what's going on inside. At first it's quiet, but seconds later, he hears some shocking words.

"Come on, let's do it one more time, for old time's sake," a male voice whispers.

"No," she cries. "Please get that gun out of my face."

The voices sound like they're coming from the back room.

"So, I can't have no more?" he asks. "You saving it all for Jamal, huh?"

Jamal, Suave thinks to himself. He wonders who this Mike guy is, and how he knows his real name.

"Please get that gun out of my face," she pleads.

Now everyone is crowded around the door, listening closely. Suave turns the knob, but it's locked. Luckily for Sincere, he never turned in his key. He pulls out his key and slides it in the door quietly. They all tiptoe through the living room.

"Fuck it, then! If I can't have none, no one will," he shouts. "Sincere, I tried. I really tried. I'm sorry to do this, but I refuse to live without you."

Boom! The single shot echoes. Suave's stomach does flip-flops. He finally makes it to the doorway of the bedroom. There he sees the shooter standing, ass naked over Sincere's body. He's standing in front of the window with his back facing them.

Suave and his man slide a bullet into the chamber simultaneously. Click, click! The noise startles the shooter. He spins around immediately. Suave and his man have beaten him to the draw. They both have their guns aimed at his head. Suave can't believe his eyes. Mike is actually Officer Jones. They lock eyes from across the room.

This punk motherfucker has ruined Suave's life. This

answers all the questions that lingered in Suave's head. Now he realizes why Officer Jones had it in for him. Now he realizes who was responsible for planting the gun on him. That cop must have been a family member of his. He tried to set him up so Suave would get sent back to prison and he could have her all to himself. Suave wonders how Sincere could betray him like that.

As Suave squeezes the trigger, he thinks of the time he's going to get for killing a cop. Sincere's mistake is going to cost him the rest of his life. He has a good mind to turn around and walk out the door. She never should have crossed him like that. He can't do that though. His pride won't let him. This is personal. Not only has Officer Jones disrespected him by fucking his woman, he just slaughtered her cold-bloodedly.

Officer Jones slyly lifts his gun in the air.

Boom! A shot sounds off. Boom! One second later, another rings off.

Officer Jones falls backwards before collapsing on the floor right next to Sincere. The window shatters. Boom! Officer Jones's gun releases once more as it falls to the floor.

Although Suave did squeeze, his shot wasn't the fatal shot. He was one second too late. By the time he squeezed, Officer Jones was already stumbling. By the time the bullet traveled across the room, there was no target. He hit nothing but the glass window.

Officer Jones knew he couldn't win. He shot himself in the head, just like the coward that he was.

Suave runs over and grabs hold of Sincere's motionless body. He squeezes her tightly. He feels like it's all his fault. If he had come a little sooner, he could have saved her. If he hadn't left her, this never would have happened.

"Please don't die," he begs as he pats her head with his shirt. The bullet pierced her temple. He can't see the bullet hole, but he can see the blood pouring rapidly down the side of her face. The thick blood has plastered her beautiful hair to her face. "Please don't die," he cries as everyone watches without a clue about what has just happened. "Please don't die!"

CHAPTER 41

Two months later

Sincere lays there unconscious. She hasn't moved once in the past two months. She's depending on the life support machine to keep her alive.

She's an awful sight. She has tubes running through her nose, her head and her heart. Her head is as big as a watermelon. Both of her eyes are puffy and blackened.

The Doctor says she isn't making the least bit of progress, but Mocha and Suave refuse to pull the plug on her.

Suave comes back into town every few days to check on her, but Mocha stays by her side day in and day out. Mocha washes her up, and grooms her. She passes the day away by singing to her and brushing the little hair Sincere has left on her swollen head. Mocha changes the color of Sincere's nail polish every other day as if she's about to get out of the bed and go somewhere.

It breaks Mocha's heart to see her like this. She can't believe that someone would do this to Sincere. Sincere would never purposely hurt anyone.

Mocha feels guilty. She just wishes she hadn't left Sincere alone in the apartment that day and this would have never happened to her.

Suave just got back into town three days ago. He sits here in the hospital room all day until visiting hours are over. Him and Mocha don't say a word to each other. They both act as if the other one isn't in the room. The hate that Suave has for Mocha has increased. He's almost sure that Mocha is the one who persuaded Sincere to creep around with Officer Jones in the first place. He wishes like hell, that it were her lying in the bed instead of Sincere.

These past months have been hell on him. It took him several weeks just to be able to step foot in the hospital. He damn near fainted at his first sight of her.

A part of him still hates her, but sympathy overpowers it. He no longer asks himself why she cheated on him, but he does ask, how could Jones do this to her? He still wonders when their affair first started.

It's so hard for him to look at her, knowing how she crossed him. He tries to put the fact of her cheating behind him, but it's extremely difficult.

Over the weeks he has acquired a drinking habit. He's drunk all day everyday. That's how he keeps his sanity. He has tried to confide in El- Amin for guidance but he's no help at all. His exact words are "The cheating ass bitch got what she deserved." Those words ripped through Suave's soul. He wanted to beat El- Amin to a pulp. The only thing that stopped him from doing so is the respect that he has for him. Not to mention, the fact that El- Amin is 100 percent right.

Suave wants to pull the plug and take her out of her misery, but he still has a little hope that she may pull through.

Right now Mocha is applying lipstick to Sincere's chapped lips, while Suave watches her with a look of disgust. A tapping on the door interrupts his hateful thoughts.

Sincere's doctor walks in wearing a long, sad face. Lumps form in Suave and Mocha's throats. They both fear the big question.

Today is Judgement Day; the day they have to make a big decision. Really, it's Suave's call. Being that Sincere has no ties with her kinship, the decision is all up to him.

"Hello, Mr. Eaddie," says the Dr. "Hi Cathy" he mumbles, as he acknowledges Mocha.

Mocha acts as if she doesn't hear him. She continues to stroke Sincere's hair.

"Hey, what's up Doc?" Suave replies in a slow whisper.

"So, have you made your decision?" the Dr. asks.

Suave hesitates before replying. "Nah, not yet Doc. I don't know what to do. That's a tough decision. I'm not prepared for it. I won't be able to live with myself, if I pull the plug, and end it for her. Just to think I stole her chances of living."

"I understand, Mr. Eaddie, but this is a decision that has to be made. To be honest with the both of you, the chances of her pulling through are 99 to 1. Her percentage is 1. We have already lost her 8 times already. And let's just say, with some miracle, she does make it -she'll be a vegetable (brain dead). She'll never walk, see or speak again. I'm not telling you to take her off of the machine, but I just want you to weigh your options. The decision is yours."

"So, she'll be a vegetable?" Suave asks.

"Yes, the bullet caused a lot of damage."

"Get out! Get out!" Mocha shouts to the Dr. "We ain't pulling the plug! Sincere is going to get up from here!" she shouts. "Just go! Get the fuck outta here!" Mocha falls to her knees and starts to cry hysterically. "Sincere, please wake up! Please! Baby, if you don't get up they're going to kill you. Please Mommy wake up. This is your last chance! You gotta get up. You gotta do this for me," she begs.

For once, Suave feels sympathy for Mocha. He's ready to cry as well, but he knows he has to be strong and hold it down. Suave wishes Officer Jones were still alive so he could kill him.

"Doc, please just give me a few days to think about it. Please," he begs.

"Ok," the doctor replies as he steps toward the door.

Just as he exits, Suave walks over to Mocha and picks her up from the floor. She falls into his arms.

"Please Suave, please don't kill her. She's all I got. Without her, there's no me. I can't live without her. If you kill her, you might as well kill me too."

"Shhh, don't cry Mo. It's going to be alright," he claims.

Those are the words that are coming out of his mouth, but he doesn't even believe them. Deep down inside, he knows it's over.

"Please Suave," she begs.

The more she begs, the harder he has to fight back the tears.

Suddenly, he can't fight anymore. The tears begin to pour from his eyes.

CHAPTER 42

One Year Later/December 15, 2005

     The place is Claymont, Delaware. The chapel is extremely crowded. Everyone watches with sympathy as El-Amin escorts Sincere down the aisle. It's taking her so long because she needs the aid of her metal walker. She's taking tiny baby steps. The bullet severely damaged her left side when it penetrated her brain. It's a miracle that she survived, but she'll never walk the same. She's totally off-balance and can't even stand up on her own.

     Just to think, the doctor told them she didn't have a chance. He also predicted that she would be brain dead if she did survive. Sincere proved him wrong. Two days after the meeting with the doctor, Sincere awoke from the coma. Mocha's prayers were answered.

     At first, they said she would never be able to walk again, but with the help of numerous specialists and countless hours of rehabilitation, she has learned to walk. She refused to give up; her determination carried her through.

     She finally makes it to the altar, where Suave is waiting patiently. She smiles a half a smile as the guests applaud her. She looks beautiful despite the paralysis of the left side of her face.

     Suave had to take her back. Watching her lay in the hospital bed, made him realize how important she is to him. He can't imagine living without her. Of course he will never be able to forget what she did to him. How could he? Her present condition is a constant reminder. He knows she crossed him, but she has paid dearly for her mistake. Hopefully he'll be able to bury the slight grudge that he has for her. He constantly asks himself if she would do the same for him if it were the other way around. He truly thinks she would.

As the music stops, Suave looks back to the first row and winks at Good Muslim (E- Boogie), who is sitting with his future wife, Aisha. Good Muslim traveled all the way to Atlanta to get back what rightfully belonged to him. Aisha is the one and only woman who has ever held the key to his heart. She was his woman before he went away. It took him all these years to realize that she was the best thing that ever happened to him, and she left him because of his neglect of her.

As for Flex, he's going to miss this special day. He got locked up sometime last year. After failing at the drug game, he went for a month-long robbing spree. They caught up with him months later. With his criminal jacket, he may never see daylight again.

Suave beat the gun charge. He fired his initial attorney and hired Tony. It took months, but he cracked the case. If Tony keeps winning cases at this rate, Johnnie Cochran may have to find another occupation.

They couldn't start the trial until Sincere was able to talk again. Once she was able to form sentences, she didn't hesitate to get on the stand to be the key witness. She had to admit that her and D'andre had an affair. It was in the courtroom that Suave got the answers to all the questions that were lingering around in his head.

It broke the jurors' hearts when Tony showed them Sincere's before and after pictures. All her exterior beauty is now a figment of the past. What used to be an attractive-looking woman is now slightly hideous looking. They all were in tears as she sat on the stand, begging and pleading to cut her lover loose. It took all the courage in the world to get up there and admit to the acts she committed.

Mocha never left her side. In fact, she learned her lesson. She has slowed down drastically. Right now, she's sitting in the second row with her fiancé. That's right –her fiancé. She pawned the ten-karat ring the rapper gave her and downgraded it to the three-karat ring that she's sporting on her left hand.

Tony proposed to her a few months ago. They met at Suave's trial. Tony asked Suave who she was. Suave tried to brush him off by telling him she's not for him, but Tony kept pushing the issue. He begged Suave to introduce him to her. At first Suave was hesitant not because of Tony, but because of the hate that he has for Mocha. Suave knows that she is a tough match for a square dude like Tony. Not only will she drain him for all his dough, but she'll also ruin his world.

Tony became so desperate that he told Suave he would take $2,000 off of his fee if he hooked them up. Suave immediately took the offer. Who ever would have imagined they would turn out to be a couple? Suave thought it would end right after the very first date. Is it love, or is it the fact that he's a prominent lawyer? Only time will tell.

"You may kiss the bride," says the minister.

The song "Don't Change" by Musiq Soul Child plays in the background.

The crowd applauds loudly as the couple begins their new life as Mr. And Mrs. Jamal "Suave" Eaddie.

ACKNOWLEDGEMENTS

I'm back once again, thanks to my loyal readers. I truly appreciate the support you all have given me with my book venture.

Halfway through this project, I must admit I was almost ready to throw in the towel, but thanks to my loved ones, I'm still in the fight. Thanks for reminding me how much of a fighter I really am. Thanks for reminding me, that when you try to do good, the devil works overtime. Thanks for reminding me that if my past obstacles didn't break me than nothing should. Those reminders kept me in the fight, and will continue to keep me in the fight -even if I have to sit on the ropes and take a beating for a few rounds. Every time that bell rings I'll run out of that corner and fight with the same courage and determination that I fought with in round one.

Win lose or draw, I'll still go down in history as a "True Fighter."

Ma, are you proud of me yet? I know I haven't made up for all the heartache I caused you, but this is only the beginning. I love you!

Much respect due to the late, great Donald Goines. Your legacy still lives on through the new generation of African American writers. Thanks for paving the way, and allowing young writers like myself to walk on top of your footprints. Over three decades later, and you still, by far are the best that did it, and got away with it.

Special shot out to "Baby U Promotions." Yusef, you the only dude I know of, who can bang 500 books a week on the ground. Hustling, is hustling!!!!

Sidi/125ᵗʰ, Hawkins/Brooklyn, Shaheed/ Manhattan, and Massamba/Queens, thanks for giving me the key to New York.

Young Face, what up!

Mikell Davis (author of Black Mafia), and Sean Timberlake (author of Second Chance), it's time to connect the dots! Mikell, there will be no more holes in my zapatos!

Khalil Sharif (author of The Lyvest Ones), where you at? Get focused my nigga! We from the Brix. We don't knock on the door, we kick it off of the hinges, feel me?

Deborah Smith (author of Ministers With White Collars and Black Secrets) keep on pushing. Your empire will be built before you know it.

Moody Holiday, from "Wild innocence" to "Portia's Secret" that's 4 in one year, just like you said you would do. Keep striving.

Wahida Clark (author of Every Thug Needs a Lady), what's happening, Believer! It soon will be over, until then, keep your pens blazing!

Kashamba Williams, (author of Blinded), remember what I told you; Stay Low! The wolves are watching, even when you think they're not.

Peace to my True 2 Life writing team:

Tariq Aaron McDaniels, I hope they ready for what you're bringing to the table. You're a quiet dude but your pen makes a lot of noise.

Nahisha McCoy, You are exactly what the book world has been screaming for.

Demond Davis, Jay Lewis and Rog Elder, no disrespect intended, One Love!!!!

Rafii, thanks for the pep talk you gave me that Sunday. You don't know how bad I needed that.

Tat and Tone, holla at ya big Cuz!

Fajr, I pray that you grow to be an obedient servant to our Lord. I surely need the blessings. Make me a proud Daddy. I love you. As Salaamu Alaikum!!!!

To my wife Charo, thanks for the support. The transition phase was rough. I couldn't have done it without you. Your encouraging words and your motivation pushed me all the way through. I love you. I dedicate to you, "__Track #14__" off of the Mario Winans Cd.

     To the Custom House on Halsey Street, thanks for keeping me fly. Always custom made, never shop off the rack! It's all about the fit. Custom made shirts and suits, even my shoes are custom made, thanks to Rafael. The gators are biting! Together ya'll make me look like a million bucks, and I ain't even worth ten cent. Ya'll gotta stop before ya'll make people hate me!

     To my big brother, El- Amin Bashir in the fed joint, in Otisville N.Y, hold it down, we gone get this book thing right so we ain't never gotta deal with that bullsh.. again. As Salaamu Alaikum!

     To my cousins, Chewy and Rahiem Summers in Trenton State, I know it's a struggle, but it's gone be alright.

     To ReBorn down Rahway, keep your head up my nigga!

     To all my dudes locked down all across the planet, stay focused and use that time wisely. Do the bid, don't let the bid do you. The game is over, it's time to set up a plan B. When you get back in the world, just stick to the script and everything else will fall in place.

     To my peoples in town and out-of-town, thanks for the support. Thanks for spreading the word that I'm "Official." "Street credibility" is everything!

     Porfirio and Swift, thanks for the hot graphics, I would love to shout out the name of the company, but I can't. I refuse to turn over my connect.

     Last but not least, may God curse the hands of the thief who broke into my car and stole my manuscript. I don't know who you are or what your intentions were, but eventually it will come to light. I flipped the script on you though. The ending of Sincerely Yours is totally different from the copy you have, so if you were thinking about copying my story or bootlegging it, YOU PLAYED YOURSELF! You slowed me down, but you can't stop me!

TRUE 2 LIFE PRODUCTIONS
Order Form

True 2 Life Productions
P.O.BOX 8722
Newark, N.J. 07108

E-mail: true2lifeproductions@verizon.net
Website: www.true2lifeproductions.com

SINCERELY YOURS ?
ISBN # 0-974-0610-2-6 $13.95
Sales Tax (6% NJ)   .83
Shipping/ Handling
Via U.S. Priority Mail $ 3.85
Total $18.63

Also by the Author:
Block Party
ISBN # 0-974-0610-1-8 $14.95
Sales Tax (6% NJ)   .89
Shipping/Handling
Via U.S. Priority Mail $3.85
Total $19.69

No Exit
ISBN # 0-974-0610-0-X $13.95
Sales Tax (6% NJ)   .83
Shipping/ Handling
Via U.S. Priority Mail $ 3.85
Total $18.63

PURCHASER INFORMATION

Name: _____

Address: _____

City: _____ State: _____ Zip Code: _____

Sincerely Yours? ___

Block Party ___

No Exit ___

HOW MANY BOOKS? _____

Make checks/money orders payable to:
True 2 Life Productions